SHADOW VALLEY

LEON JANE

BARRAMUNDI PUPLISHING

barrapublishing@gmail.com

Also by Leon Jane:

Stormbird

For Carissa and Jacinta and for their love of books.

Mary had a little cat,

Its coat was black as coal,

And every time the cat left her,

It ate away her soul.   – L.J.

Prologue

Her eyes burned as she looked directly at the sun. She was trying to dry her tears by staring into the rays of the sun, but it wasn't working. She gripped the long grass beside the freshly laid mound of dirt and screamed at the top of her lungs. There was no one around, at least no one there that could answer her cries. Why did her life take this journey, why was she left here, alone and cold in Shadow Valley?

A single butterfly wing, iridescent blue on one side and charcoal black on the other, danced across the grass field tossed about by the stiff breeze. It moved like it had once before when it was attached and when the butterfly was alive. Now in its 'second life' it seemed to meander across the field, this time not stopping at the occasional meadow flower but rolling and tumbling past them. In one last gust it flipped and spun dark side up and pinned itself to her ankle. She gazed down at it vacantly and peeled it off carefully, protecting its fragile remains from the wind. She found the coloured side and played with the wing between her fingers against the sunlight, making the iridescences shimmer. A tear rolled down her cheek at the thought of its beauty and of the butterfly's death. To her, right now, it made sense but she didn't want to understand it, she didn't want to reason with the premise of the circle of life, that there was beauty in death. She didn't want to believe it. Why should she? She held the wing up high and let it go, she watched it get picked up by the wind, dance in the sky, spin and twirl before vanishing out of sight.

Mary lay back on the soft grass hoping that it would slowly grow over her body. She hoped that the grass would bury her and drag her down through the earth to reach her soul mate. There she hoped she would be with him forever. This would never happen. Mary missed his soft kisses and just the reassuring comfort of his presence. It was now all gone. Her eyes began to weep again just thinking of this and a lump formed in her throat. Tears flowed freely from her burning eyes. How did her life come to this abrupt emptiness, how could she go on? She wished her memory of the last couple of weeks would die but as she closed her eyes it all came flooding back like a bad nightmare.

Chapter One

BANG! A timber tray of food smashed across the hard, slate floor of the castle dungeon. It was like clockwork at exactly the same time every day. Her one and only meal was delivered personally by the princess at midday. There was no communication between the princess and her captive, just a glare, the usual delivery of the food across the floor and a slam of her cell door. The encounter was promptly over with the locks on the cage door quickly secured.

Day in, day out the meal never differed. It usually consisted of cold leftovers from the royal staff breakfast. This was a direct order by the princess that everyone in the castle had to eat before all the prisoners. The only difference between this prisoner's meal and the other prisoner's meals is that theirs were substantial and warm and hers was cold and stingy. Also the other prisoners were able to congregate in a mess hall and eat together under guard. Mary thought the reason her meal was so different to the other captors was because they needed their strength for the hard labor that they had to endure whereas Mary had never left the confinements of her prison cell walls. She was quite weak, pale and slightly gaunt. Her sad disposition was accentuated by the way her pale face, framed by dirty blonde hair, displayed her misery as her cornflower blue eyes staring vacantly into the darkness.

Mary pulled her dirty, thick dress underneath her as she sat down beside the timber food tray. She usually sat on the floor waiting for her food as she was too weak to stand for long periods. It was more convenient for her to gather up all the scraps anyway. She didn't care for the disrespect that it showed the princess. For all she knew the princess probably thought she was crippled, otherwise she would have seen additional punishment, like a public flogging. She was glad she was spared that humiliation. She wiped her already greasy hands on her dress but that did little to clean them. In the dim light of her cell she started to gather the food together and try to make a meal out of it.

She looked up momentarily as a black form slinked its way towards her from out of the shadows. Samuel proudly marched over to join her as she sorted through the food scraps. The only luxury that Mary was allowed was her pet cat. He was now poking his head out from under Mary's dilapidated bed and was sniffing the air at the mess of food. Mary made sure Samuel ate first. Mary ate what little was left. She thought if Samuel were to go hungry and get sick then he may very well leave her here all on her own. Then Mary would see no reason to go on. Samuel gave Mary her strength and will to live. He was all she knew. With each day the memories of her past life were slowly slipping from her fragile mind. Samuel kept her sane.

Samuel was a striking looking cat. His green eyes pierced through his black fur and captivated whoever he gazed at. His coat was shiny and well kept. He wore a braided leather collar, tan in colour with a smoky glass charm that Mary had attached to it many years ago when he was a kitten. She thought it made him look smart.

His devotion to Mary was like no other. He would often go missing for days, much to Mary's concern, only to return with a small bird or field mouse that he had killed. He would promptly drop it at her feet and look up at her with his deep eyes and give her a small meow. She thought he was trying to say, "there you go, eat up." He was worried about her. The guards always laughed at how 'the scrawny cat' took pity on her.

Mary spent many hours laying there and stroking his fur, scratching under his chin, just gazing into the darkness. She wondered about why she was there in the dungeon. She had known a reason why once upon a time but she has forgotten now because her memory faded from being captive for so long. She wondered if all the royalty was as mean as Princess Margaret, she had heard whispers and rumors in the corridors that there was a

King, and that he was quite a generous man. She wondered why she had never seen him. For all she knew though it was just a fairytale that others pinned their hopes and dreams on in order to keep their sanity. She thought they gave themselves a false sense of security that someday the kind King may set them free. Samuel was Mary's only savior.

"Don't worry Samuel," she said looking at him as he now rubbed his body against her thigh, "she is looking after me." He carried on purring in anticipation of some food. Mary's comment was referring to the princess and how she treated her as she looked at the mess of food still spread across the cell floor. Samuel continued rubbing against her lovingly as he purred. His tail stood erect and whipped around playfully at the end, catching her matted, dirty blonde hair with each flick.

"After all," Mary continued, "she is my sister."

Chapter Two

"Scale of dragon, eye of newt, nail of sloth," recited the young apprentice as he dropped each ingredient into a bubbling cauldron. With each ingredient the bubbling eruptions from within the cauldron seemed to get more wildly violent.

"A lock of troll hair, a pinch of fairy dust, a drop of lizard tears," continued the wizard's apprentice.

The noises must have awoken the master of the house as the wooden door burst open. "What on second earth are you doing?" bellowed the grumpy old wizard as he entered his laboratory, scratching his long, wispy, grey beard.

"Um, just experimenting sir Mertane, master, sir," hesitated his nephew.

"You might be related to me Varn, but that is no excuse to waste rare ingredients!" cursed Mertane.

Varn swung around hurriedly and tried to tidy up the loose ingredients which were all over the wooden work bench. He was quite young for an apprentice wizard but had shortcut some of the learning schools and training because he was the nephew of the kingdom's wizard, The Great Mertane.

"Leave those things alone, I'll put them back, you might lose them," instructed Mertane. His aged hands darted out from his thick cloak sleeves pointing at all the jars, satchels and loose ingredients as though he was trying to gather them all up from a distance. Mertane was afraid that he would never find the wizardry ingredients when he would need them, especially if he relied on his young apprentice to correctly return them. "You need to leave your learning or 'experimenting' as you put it for when you go to Master Wizard College."

"Yes sir," replied Varn.

"Leave the application of the spells until you have read and studied them completely," guided Mertane. "This will ensure you don't get yourself in a dangerous situation."

"Yes sir," mumbled Varn, in a melodramatic tone as he turned away from Mertane, who kept barking instructions and advice. He was about to get on with the job of packing up when he accidently knocked over a large jar of worm's guts. The jar promptly rolled across the wooden table bumping other ingredients on its journey. It seemed to bounce off the end of the table as Varn dove to stop it falling. Mertane quickly grabbed the scruff of his nephew's training cloak and held him back. With a plop the entire jar disappeared from sight into the gurgling surface of the liquid within the cauldron.

"Get down!" Mertane shouted.

Time seemed to go in slow motion as the pair dropped to the ground and shielded themselves from the inevitable. Mertane managed to drag a nearby chair with his free arm and place it in between themselves and the erupting cauldron.

The blast was a sheer glow followed by a succession of small deafening explosions. The dark room seemed to glow brilliant white, like the midday sun. Hot liquid was thrown about the room like they were in a giant washing machine. Luckily the chair protected them. When it was over steam rose from everywhere and it smelt like fermented footballer's socks. It was disgusting. Varn dared not speak.

Mertane was dazed, he couldn't believe his eyes. His entire laboratory was reduced to a pile of steaming muck. It took him years to get his laboratory to how he wanted it and within seconds his young apprentice had destroyed it. He was about to open his mouth and explode himself, to give Varn a dressing down, when something took his words, his seething fury and rage instantly switched off. His jaw dropped.

"I'll do anything to make up for this sir, I promise, I beg of you please forgive me," pleaded Varn.

"Quiet child," instructed Mertane.

Mertane was now mesmerized by the glowing amulet which he saw in the reflection of a broken mirror before him. The amulet hung from a chain around his own neck. Mertane remembered how it once shone as a small blue orb but for many, many years it sat dormant hanging around his neck. Now the blue orb was faintly glowing again, not to its full beauty but it was as though the blast had just awoken it.

When Mertane next spoke Varn couldn't believe the words he uttered, "Varn, I believe you have just done something for which is both extraordinary and life changing." Mertane believed that for what Varn had just done would make him forever indebted to him.

Chapter Three

She stroked his long, wiry, grey beard. She used her manicured fingernails to tease out any knotted hair. Suddenly he groaned and woke in a coughing fit.

"Now, now daddy," coaxed Princess Margaret in a soothing voice. "You must rest if you are going to get better."

As the king gathered himself his coughing subsided and he tried to sit up in his bed. Princess Margaret helped him by placing extra pillows behind his head. She sat patiently beside him and waited for him to wake properly. He probably wouldn't have known that she was there unless she had spoken as his bed was expansive. The four poster bed commanded the room with its carved oak pillars framing the thick linen sheets which seemed to spill over the sides of the bed like fabric glaciers.

"How long have you been here, my love?" he asked of his daughter.

"I am always here for you, daddy," she replied.

King Henry patted his daughter's hand in thanks. His weighty hand was pale, spotted with solar keratosis and covered in pronounced blue veins which was a stark contrast from her small, smooth and blemish free one. Her hands looked like they had never done one moment of hard work in all their twenty-six years. For a moment he believed he was the luckiest king of all the land, then the shadows in his heart pulled tight and he gulped trying to drown the pain of his memories. He had something to tell his daughter, he thought this was the best time to relieve himself of the guilt in his past. He knew his time on this earth was fast coming to an end.

"What did the doctors say, daddy?" Princess Margaret asked.

"I am afraid they bear no good news," King Henry said matter-of-factly. It didn't surprise him how easy it was to say. He had been ready for the doctor's bad news for quite some time.

"Oh daddy, what am I to do?" cried Princess Margaret. "You can't leave me," she said selfishly.

"Please, Margret, I must tell you something," King Henry said. "It pains me to explain my troubled past, but it shall be wonderful news for you."

"What do you mean, daddy?" she asked, looking surprised.

"Well love, you shall not be alone, when I finally pass," he said, "you will have help to rule this land."

Princess Margaret raised her eyebrows, her forehead began to perspire and her right eye twitched. King Henry could not see this as he was vacantly looking forward as he spoke. Although his eyesight was poor he was too ashamed to look her in the eye.

"You have a sister," King Henry stated. He waited for Princess Margaret's reaction before he explained about his affair while married to the late queen. Such an affair bore another child who was whisked off to another land before anyone would find out. This child grew up in a poor rural farm. The king had left the foster parents quite an amount of money, a king's ransom you could say, which was secretly put in place to make sure the child was always looked after. After this the king had to lose ties with her upbringing, he thought it was for her own safety.

Princess Margaret turned around and walked over to a bedside dresser. Upon the dresser sat a silver serving platter with silver goblet and vessel. She poured the cool liquid from the vessel into the silver goblet and returned to the side of the bed. Now King Henry was staring at Princess Margaret in the eyes, he was searching for a reaction, anything, but no emotion was to be given from Princess Margaret.

"Here daddy, I made you a soothing drink to help your sore throat," she said.

"And about what you have just learnt?" the King said in concern with eyebrows raised.

"Shh, shh, just drink this and things will be all better," she placed the rim of the goblet at the king's lips, tipping it upwards gently as he slowly sipped the cool liquid down.

She waited until his eyes grew heavy, his focus on her blurred. "Now," she said, "such nonsense that you speak will never leave this room."

She wasn't sure if he had heard her last sentence, but she was certain of one thing, that King Henry would be dead by the time she left his quarters as the poison made its way to his weak heart.

Chapter Four

Varn swept the slate floor of the laboratory with a heavy bristled broom. The bits of broken glass crunched and clinked against each other. Dust and a dank odor hung in the air. Varn coughed and almost dry retched from the toxic atmosphere that his wayward experiment created. He would have normally complained about doing such horrid and dirty tasks but because this mess was his doing he was wise to keep his frustrations hidden.

The spell that Varn was trying to perfect was one that he was trying to impress his master with. With all the excitement about the glowing amulet Varn was happy that Mertane didn't question him further about it. Varn was sure it was going to work, he nearly had it working at Master Wizard College, and even there though he was keeping it secret from his teacher and other students.

Varn was a wiry, sixteen year old boy with thick greasy black hair offset by pale white complexion. He literally stood out from his peers because he stood a whole head height above them. They jeered at him and called him the 'Albino Giraffe' because of his height and his complexion or 'Golden Wizard Boy' because of his relationship with Master Wizard Mertane, but it didn't bother him. He was lucky that he did possess a natural wizard craft talent and he also had the passion to learn. These two character traits kept him focused on learning and becoming a brilliant wizard and also kept him resilient to the taunts and negativity that sometimes blanketed Kingsgate like a winter's fog.

As he kept cleaning he was amazing how far the gunk was thrown during the explosion. Varn was equally amazed at all the cracks and crevices in the laboratory that the gunk had found itself. It took Varn what seemed like an eternity to get the place looking half clean. Just as he was about to tackle the last corner of the laboratory Mertane entered the room. The amulet which hung from around his neck still glowed faintly.

"I am going to have to look through the books for a spell that creates a fresh smell, you know like broken pine needles on the forest floor or like the first rain on a spring meadow," Mertane complained. "And before you start to lecture me about not being able to produce any magic for self-benefit, I am sure you'll agree that a fresh scent potion would do us all the world of good."

Mertane was starting to rant and rave again, but he was right. The bad smell produced from the explosion was starting to give poor Varn a headache. Mertane watched as Varn scraped up the last bucket load of broken bits of timber, wet paper and smashed glass.

As Mertane watched Varn finish cleaning he thought that it was time that he told his young apprentice the story behind the amulet around his neck. "Varn son, you have done enough," instructed Mertane. "Please rest now as I tell you the truth behind this glowing amulet."

In the distance bells could be heard chiming. It was an unusual time of the day for bells to be ringing. "Mertane sir, have I forgotten to record in your diary of an important church service?" Varn asked. As the amulet glowed brighter around Mertane's neck he looked across at the boy with shock in his eyes, "No Varn, you have not missed anything, those bells are not from the church, they are from the castle." he explained clutching at the amulet and looking at it in disbelief, "I am afraid they are special chimes intended to tell the townsfolk of Kingsgate that royalty has died!"

Chapter Five

He gently kissed her dry cheek as she slept. A morning ray of light slowly traced its way across the floor from a crack high in the wall. This was her only natural light. He kissed her again, careful not to startle her, although the links in his neck charm rattled which caused her to stir.

Her lips pursed and she opened her mouth slightly and groaned. She was dreaming. Her dreams were of riding across a meadow, speckled with wild flowers, on the back of a white stallion. The wind whipped the stallion's brilliant white mane about as she could see a bright light in the distance. She felt warm. She felt safe. The light got brighter and then she woke. The ray of sunlight had made its way across her face and now was shining brightly in her eyes. Samuel nudged her with his head.

"Good morning to you too Samuel," she said sleepily. "If only you could see my dreams."

He purred and nudged her with his head some more as she sat up. He was looking forward to his morning pat and scratch under the chin.

"It must be close to breakfast time," Mary said, "as I can hear your stomach growling, or is that mine?"

Mary didn't bother getting up off the floor until after breakfast was served. She thought that it ended up on the floor anyway so she didn't bother moving. This was her only bit of retribution. She thought the princess might have scolded her if she ever found out that she didn't even make an effort to stand while breakfast was served. Mary didn't care, how much worse off could her life get? If only she knew what would unfold for her this morning.

Mary heard the usual clatter of the other prisoners being served. The usual gripes and moans from her inmates that she never saw gave her some comfort that her misery was not unique and that she was not alone down here. Apart from having Samuel with her though, she was truly alone.

A guard made his way to her cell door. He rattled the keys on his large steel key ring before finding the right one. The cell door screeched open and banged against the stone wall as he threw it open. No princess today. Something was wrong. Mary grabbed Samuel to protect him and he huffed as he was startled and his breath was quickly taken from his chest. Mary loosened her grip slightly when she realized she had too much of a hold on poor Samuel but she still held him securely.

"The prisoner must stand!" bellowed the guard. Guards never addressed a prisoner directly and only barked orders to them in second person. This was to show authority and more over to show that the prisoner was never an equal.

"The prisoner must stand!" repeated the guard. Mary sat still, mostly out of sheer fright. Both she and Samuel looked wide eyed up at him from the floor.

The guard threw himself at Mary and grabbed a large tuft of hair from the back of her head. She screamed in pain as he dragged her from the cell by her hair. Samuel hissed then caterwauled with fright and jumped from Mary to hide in the shadows.

"Samuel!" cried Mary as she kicked and screamed trying to hold her weight off her hair with both her arms. The guard dragged Mary backwards out of her cell and down the dungeon hallway, further and further away from Samuel. Tears rolled from her eyes and made dirty streams across her cheeks as she thought that she may never see Samuel again.

Chapter Six

"Is the prisoner contained?" demanded Princess Margaret. Behind a large oak table, she sat in a luxurious high back chair that was cherry red oak with a mirror polished finish. A velvet blue fabric which covered the thick but plush padding was tacked over the seat and armrests. It was so comfortable that Princess Margaret struggled not to nod off. But she dared not to, she had important instructions to issue this morning.

"Yes, your majesty," replied Princess Margaret's personal servant, Lady Jane, in a quietly spoken manner. She was a thin middle aged woman who although looked plain and drab was quite a powerful member of the royal family as she was head of all the servants. She knew how to make the kingdom run like clockwork and was well admired by the late king.

"Good, now go and make sure the prisoner is prepared, ready for tonight's ceremony," instructed Princess Margaret. Lady Jane bowed her head, her grey hair defied gravity and stayed in position. She always wore it in a traditional bun which accentuated her sense of importance and wisdom. She turned and made her way from Princess Margaret's quarters. She moved briskly as she was in a hurry to get out the door when Princess Margaret barked one last order. "Oh and Jane, I want nothing to go wrong tonight, otherwise you can spend some time in that newly, emptied dungeon cell."

The threat was enough to make Lady Jane skip off in a hurry without answering. Princess Margaret didn't mind the insignificant disobedience that Lady Jane just displayed by not answering her as it meant the message gave a final sting, as it was intended to do. She loved watching her subordinates squirm, she loved preying on them and keeping them inline much like how her pet scorpions danced around their prey before they gave the fatal stab of their tail.

"Lord James, Lord James! Answer me at once," demanded Princess Margaret in a whining and grating voice as she moved position in the chair trying to place herself snuggly. She turned her head to look out the window over the royal gardens that surrounded the palace. The royal gardeners were busy pruning the roses and maintaining the gardens. They worked hard from sunrise to sunset with little time for rest. It was a much sought after tenure within the kingdom. They were sweating, which she despised.

Moments later Lord James appeared in the doorway. He bowed his head and answered her, "yes, your majesty." Lord James was an older gentleman in his later years. He was the late King Henry's second cousin. He performed many duties in Kingsgate but most importantly he was commander of the royal army which also made him in charge of palace security. He was once a heroic soldier on the battlefield, but now because of his age and stoutly disposition his tactical wisdom and leadership was much more important being led from the royal chambers than on top of a battle horse.

"Lord James, I am sure you are aware of the ceremony tonight to celebrate my father, King Henry's life," she said.

"Yes, your majesty," Lord James replied knowing too well of King Henry's funeral.

"Well tonight there will be three celebrations," Princess Mary stated.

"Yes, your majesty?" questioned Lord James.

"Yes, three celebrations," she continued, "firstly it will be my daddy's funeral, secondly and most importantly it will be my coronation as Queen Margaret and thirdly we will celebrate with the hanging of my first prisoner."

Lord James' mouth dropped, he was dumbfounded. He knew Princess Margaret would eventually become queen but this usually took months of organizing. Coronation of a queen most definitely never took place on the same day of a King's funeral, let alone in the same ceremony. A king's wake was respectfully observed for days if not months.

"If I may ask, your majesty, why do we complicate this already busy ceremony with a hanging?" he asked, frowning and turning to look out the window so as to not show her his displeasure.

"It's not complicated Lord James. The people are sad, they need a hanging to uplift their spirits," she explained. "I implore you to head the Proclamation at once, we mustn't dilly dally," she said sternly looking towards him.

"Indeed your majesty, may I ask which prisoner bequests their presence to your auspicious event?" asked Lord James, turning and now facing Princess Margaret.

"Why, none other than the prisoner who calls itself Mary," retorted Princess Margaret.

Chapter Seven

As Lady Jane made her way to the maid's chambers she quickly wiped the tears that tried to escape from her eyes. She was usually a tough woman but getting used to Princess Margaret's taunts was going to be a big learning curve. Lady Jane may have had a small disposition and slight frame but she was very strong at heart.

As she arrived at the maid's chambers she was greeted by the Chief Maid who was expecting her. The Chief Maid's day was also turned upside down with the arrival of an unsolicited delivery.

"Your lots in that store room," she said pointing towards the corner of the room. "You'll find all you need in there to perform your miracle."

Lady Jane thanked the Chief Maid and walked over to the store room door. As she stepped inside the store room she was surprised to see a burly guard standing there.

"Guard, you are dismissed!" Lady Jane ordered.

"I have strict instructions not to leave sight of the prisoner," replied the guard.

"Stand outside the store room, there is only one entry here, she'll not escape," said Lady Jane.

"No!" shouted the guard.

"Do so and I'll double your allowance," bribed Lady Jane.

The guard sensed that this wasn't a false bribe as he knew that the royal assistants took care of the workers allowance. The allowance wasn't seen as an income as you were blessed to serve the royal family, however workers couldn't survive on love alone so they received a pension to ensure that there was no mutiny amongst the ranks.

"Yes, madam," the guard said and he left the room.

"That is Lady Jane to you, guard," she corrected.

"Ah, yes, I beg your pardon, Lady Jane," stumbled the guard as he slinked out of the store room.

Lady Jane turned to the center of the store room. There was a large box shape which was covered with white cloth. Lady Jane removed the cloth to reveal a square cage that was too small to stand up in. At the bottom of the cage, curled into a ball and quietly sobbing was Mary.

Mary's head hurt and it was throbbing. She almost blacked out from the pain of being dragged along from her hair. She was certainly too distracted by the cruelty to be aware of how she ended up in this confined space and in the maid's store room.

Mary just noticed the brighter light as Lady Jane had lifted the white cloth from the cage to expose her. She winced from the glare and shielded her eyes. Lady Jane let Mary take her time to get used to her surroundings, for her eyes to adjust to the light. Beside the cage was a box which contained clean clothes and various sized bottles. Beside that was a short wooden barrel with a wide opening and filled with steaming, hot water.

"I am not here to hurt you," said Lady Jane. "I am here to clean you up," she said as she opened the cage door and held out her hand, like an olive branch, trying to coax her out. Mary was surprised, firstly by being spoken to directly and secondly for being able to bath. Both things she couldn't remember having had done to her for quite some time.

"Wha..., What for, Miss Lady Jane?" asked Mary. Lady Jane was surprised that she had heard her scold the guard and was kind enough to address her properly. This was something that a prisoner had never done before. Lady Jane sensed that this was no ordinary prisoner.

"Well," Lady Jane said, "there is a celebration tonight and you are attending." Lady Jane opened the cage door and helped the timid girl out onto the hard store room floor.

"Why me?" asked Mary.

Lady Jane found it hard to prevent the lump in her throat forming as she lied to Mary. "Come on, off with these clothes I have to get you ready. Princess Margaret has asked for you as you are her special guest of honor."

Chapter Eight

Beyond the thick woods which wrap around the southern edge of the kingdom of Kingsgate lies a quaint rural village. This village produces most of the Kingsgate's food needs. It's protected from conquering from other kingdoms by its natural barrier, the valley in which it is situated.

The former king and queen loved to visit the valley and celebrate with the village folk during harvest festivals. The townsfolk loaded carts with fruits and vegetables and the carts were decorated with flowers. The produce looked like it was floating on flower beds. Horses were washed, brushed and garnished with ribbons and more flowers and also the workers were all dressed and decorated in the finest clothes. The finest specimens of each type of livestock, like cows, sheep, goats and pigs were also washed, dressed and presented. They all paraded along, in front of the staged king and queen, past the town's center square behind a marching band which belted out thunderous songs. The festivities could last for weeks at a time depending on how well the season was. It was quite a happy time.

The queen loved the valley and its natural beauty. Rock walls which faced the castle of Kingsgate rose up quite steeply and caught the clouds with their rain, making it a very fertile place. There was a waterfall which cascaded over the wall, causing a mist and usually a rainbow. The waterfall fed the river below which snaked its way through the valley. These valley walls, or cliffs, gave the village its official name of Queenscliff, but the locals call it by its treasured name, Shadow Valley.

In winter Shadow Valley got bitterly cold in the afternoon as the sun's rays were shaded by the high cliff walls. It usually harbored crisp microclimates which help yield bumper crops of grapes for wine making. Wine was prized by the king therefore it was only drunk by royalty. It was also a valuable trading commodity between neighboring kingdoms. Though with these restrictions it didn't stop a black market of alcohol being sold and drunk, but it did stop public drunkenness, which would have resulted in instant imprisonment, even with such a happy and generous ruling king.

Usually sunny and warm this time of year there was a sense of an early winter upon the land. And today was no exception as it was a particularly cold day, it was the end of harvest, the leaves on the grape vines were starting to turn brown and fall. Little did the busy workers of Shadow Valley know that the crisp chill in the air this evening may as well have been from the slice of a double edged sword, for when they realize that one of their own will be sacrificed in front of them, it too would cut them deeply.

"Hold on Varn!" warned Mertane, "we're nearly there."

"But aren't we going the wrong way, we are heading in the opposite direction to the castle, shouldn't we see which royalty has died?" questioned Varn. At this time of the day his head was spinning. His morning had been turned upside down and that's not including the explosion in Mertane's den which he had caused. He still had not grasped the idea that Mertane half explained to him about the glowing amulet which was linked to royalty with some sort of dark shroud of mystery over its origins.

"Oh do hold on Varn, I don't have time to cast a repair spell if you fall off, this is the right way and we don't have time to find out who has died as I fear by the day's end we will be all in grave danger if we don't find more answers to this glowing amulet," warned Mertane as Varn clutched onto the back of his thick cloak. Their horse grunted in complaint as it carried both their weight. It too wasn't used to such a rushed journey this early in the morning. It was happily eating chaff this morning in its warm stable and wanted to be back there.

Their horse galloped and puffed down the winding forest track. The path seemed to be getting tighter and more closed in as they got deeper into the forest. The horse started to complain further by turning its head, snarling and glaring at Mertane under taught bridle and reins. If it could it would have bitten Mertane. A wizard's horse wasn't cut out for this hard labor and was letting him know about it with its deathly glares.

Just when he thought the horse was about to lock up its legs and throw them off over the front Mertane saw a change in scenery up ahead. Shots of jutting sunlight sliced through the canopy and stabbed the widening path. The trees that lined the path gradually fell away until a vast field stretched out in front of them. It was beginning to appear more rural to Varn.

Mertane pulled back on the reins to slow the horse down, which he neighed loudly in relief. Varn could now get a proper look at his surroundings. It was a beautiful scene up ahead, a rolling tapestry of fields flanked at either side by high, grey rocked cliff faces. The morning sun cast long shadows from the pine trees which had been planted alongside the fields to act as windbreaks. Their shadows looked like giant fingers clutching at the crops keeping them safe. "Wow, this place is beautiful," gasped Varn. "I've never seen this place, I didn't know it existed."

As the horse slowed to a trot Mertane leant back and explained, "Well we're here boy, hopefully we can find the answers to save Kingsgate here in Shadow Valley."

Chapter Nine

"Yes, yes, yes!" shrieked Princess Margaret as she rolled around naked on her royal bed which was layered in lavish jewelry. She thought that cold precious metals, gemstones and coins pressed against her naked skin felt soothing. As she writhed around the sunlight from a nearby window was reflected up by the gems and thrown around the room. Flecks of yellow, green and red shimmered light like a mirror ball across medieval tapestries which adorned the walls. The closer and harder these treasures pressed into her body, to her being, the more ecstatic she felt. For her it was like being closer to God. It was greed, gluttony, avarice and lust all rolled into one, literally.

Earlier that day she had ordered the contents of the king's safe, a staggering amount of jewelry, to be delivered to her room. These jewels had been locked up safely and hadn't seen daylight ever since the queen had passed away, even Princess Margaret was too young to have seen them before. The king was embarrassed by the quantity and value of the treasures but deemed them a necessary evil only to be used for trade in times of hardship, like if the kingdom was struck by drought and famine. Luckily this had never happened due to their natural treasure of Shadow Valley, but nonetheless King Henry always liked its insurance value.

The jewels had been mostly acquired during the troubled times when neighboring kingdoms, under rule by oppressive leaders, decided to try and conquer their land and its people, together with their lives and their treasures. Most of these oppressive leaders had exhausted their own kingdom's resources and it was a last vigilant act for them to survive by trying to raid their neighbors. King Henry was able to defend from these attacks, capture and imprison their leaders and welcome the new regions and people under his greater kingdom. Securing their jewels was one of the first necessary evils.

"Oh, yes, yes, yes daddy!" snorted Princess Margaret like a pig at its feeding trough. "Where have you been my whole life?" she questioned the jewels as she let fists full of gold chains snake down her arms while laying on her back, clutching them toward the ceiling.

Her smile beamed. She was beginning to love the spoils of being the ruler of Kingsgate. Forget all the nitty gritty, day to day dealings that took her precious time. The insignificant, winging and whining from the people of the land and how poor they were, or how sick they were. Decisions for this and decisions for that, all of which now paled into insignificance. This is what it was all about, this is where she could be forever.

Her mind wandered. What of her sister, it wasn't her fault that she was born a bastard, out of wedlock. It wasn't her fault that she was the product of the king's adultery. It wasn't her fault that she was hidden away. 'Maybe she could share the kingdom with me,' thought the princess, 'after all she is of my blood.' But she scowled at the thought. 'Her blood isn't blue, her blood is impure,' she reasoned, 'my decision is right, my decision is final.'

"Servants!" screamed Princess Margaret still laying on her back with the jewelry covering her just in the right areas barely containing her modesty, still with her fists full of gold chains. The room's large oak doors creaked inwards and in rushed two servants with their heads bowed.

"Yes, your excellency?" asked the servants in unison, with their heads forever down.

"Take these chains to Lady Jane at once, give her my instructions to make me a dress from them for tonight, and if it isn't the most stunning dress that eyes have ever seen then we will be having four hangings tonight, not just one!"

Chapter Ten

He slinked along the passageways making sure he stayed hidden in the shadows. His eyes darting back and forward continuously checking that it was safe to proceed. If he heard a noise he would stop, wait quietly, his sensors sharpened, then when danger passed he would continue on his way.

It seemed like an eternity but he continued his search. After advancing several flights of stairs he came to a passageway in the castle that opened up to a large hall. This section of the castle was quite different from the areas that he had just explored. The walls were adorned with thick tapestries which depicted scenes of cheerful royalty in historic moments of time. The ceiling was painted with religious scenes and it was all framed with gold guided carvings around the perimeter. There was a tasteful dotting of either mirror polished timber furniture or detailed marble statues along the lengths of the cavernous room. 'There must be something really important here,' he thought.

He made his way along one side of the room and stopped short of what appeared to be a doorway. He heard voices. He slowly crept along the base of the huge timber door which was slightly ajar. The voices grew louder, it sounded like an argument.

"Yes your majesty, but do we really need to see two deaths in one day? Perhaps your majesty should show her people feast, song and dance?" pleaded Lord James.

"Do you want to join the prisoner and swing like a chandelier from the neck?" she threatened.

"No your majesty, I only suggest alternatives to best enhance your welcoming with the people that shall adore you," reasoned Lord James.

"It would be wise of you, Lord James, to suggest to me what I expect, not what you think. Otherwise you know your fate," warned Princess Margaret.

"Yes your majesty," answered Lord James

"Good, now update me with the progress of tonight's festivities, give me some good news," she demanded.

He heard the bickering but was intrigued with these 'night festivities'. He rounded the base of the entrance door and slipped into the room without them seeing him. He slinked over to the side of the room and hid behind a tall gold gilded dresser. He couldn't see them and he needed to get a higher vantage point. He sprung to the top of the dresser, landing with quiet stealth and hiding beside a large glass vase. The vase was filled with hundreds of roses, all in different stages of bloom and every single one a different colour. He was happy here, he could see them talking and he could dart behind the vase if he got nervous.

They were at the end of a four poster bed, both seated and both on opposite sides. "Well, your majesty will be pleased to learn that your da...," Lord James stopped himself from slipping up and committing a royal blasphemy, "that the late King Henry's body has been prepared and is ready for sending off."

"Continue," she ordered, raising an eyebrow at the potential slip up.

"Yes, your majesty, the dressmakers are in the final stages of your majesty's dress, and might I add, what a breathtaking thing of beauty it is," reassured Lord James.

"It's expected," retorted Princess Margaret.

"Well yes," continued Lord James, heavily gulping before he continued, hoping any news would please her majesty, "and the prisoner, Mary, has been prepared, and is being guarded in the assistant's quarters, she is none the wiser to her impending hanging."

Princess Margaret's face beamed a wicked smile but it quickly turned into a frown as she whipped her head around to see why a large vase full of roses smashed to the floor from a dresser.

Samuel had been sprung. The last words that he heard from Lord James made his body stiffen and he stood, bolt upright on all fours. His shift in weight was an uncontrollable reaction and resulted in the large vase he was hiding behind being pushed over the edge of the dresser.

He had no time to waste and in a blackened dash he sprinted out the door, with his ears pinned back. All that he heard before he was beyond the large room and down the stairs was a shrill scream of, "kill that disgusting rat!"

Chapter Eleven

Small farm houses and rolling fields of crops and livestock gave way to more densely populated buildings and structures as Mertane and Varn made their way towards Shadow Valley's central district. The closer they got to the center of town the busier it got. Mertane was hoping he would find who he was looking for by asking around at the Shadow Valley markets which were at the heart of the town.

They slowed to a trot as they finally reached the outskirts of the town center, it was far too busy now to lead a horse through the hustle of people and carts. They both couldn't help but notice the long stares and glares that they were receiving from the town's folk. Out of towners, especially visitors from Kingsgate were always unwelcome. They were seen as vagrants who exploited the hard toils of the people of Shadow Valley. It was hard for them to see any benefit of being ruled by Kingsgate because Shadow Valley was always prosperous and very nearly mostly self-sufficient.

After they dismounted, Mertane tethered the horse to a rail, without discussion he gave a lad some change to look after their horse. He seemed to be trustworthy as it looked as though the boy made a living from minding other horses also tethered there. Mertane and Varn continued on foot.

They followed one of the arteries of the town which was a narrow but busy alley way also lined with stalls and shops. This alley leads to the main event, the main attraction of the town, the Shadow Valley Markets. As they squeezed past numerous vendors and town folk they finally made it. There in front of them was a spectacle, it was a maze of stalls and tables covered with fruit, vegetables and meats grown in the valley. It was quite a sight for young Varn, his first time in Shadow Valley and in the markets. It was a feast for his sensors. The mountains of fruits, sometimes spilling over the tables, were of all the colours of the rainbow, the fruit was flanked by neatly stacked mounds of seasonal vegetables each with their own fresh odor. Stall holders bellowed out at the tops of their voices their specials for the day.

Mertane looked across towards the back of the markets, looking for a familiar corridor, searching for a known exit. All the while Varn was finding it hard to keep up with Mertane. His nose was in overload, the smells coming from large copper pots broiling with stews as steam curtained the passageways. "Do keep up Varn," barked Mertane, "I can't lose precious time having to backtrack to find you."

Sweaty shoppers gave sharp glares as they pushed their way past in a hasty manner. Varn found it mesmerizing as he watched Mertane from behind. His purple cloak looked like it was being forever swallowed by a sea of hemp gowns in all the shades of brown and grey worn by the locals. Varn was beginning to feel nauseous with the rolling swell of people in front of him and with the smells of food being cooked all around which now seem to mix into one unpleasant smell.

With such a busy place, where bartering was common and stall holders were vying for your precious money there was also an element of danger and there were things Varn wished he hadn't seen. Varn cringed at the sight of the game which he could not recognize which was stripped of its skin, hanging upside down on racks and dripping with blood, flies and maggots. His stomach churned and kicked as his nostrils drew in its stench. As he looked the other way his eyes were drawn to a beggar woman sitting on the ground, holding up a tin for your charity. She was mumbling incoherent gibberish and reeking of urine as a stream of yellow fluid trailed from underneath her, staining the cobblestone. The charm of the markets had worn off quickly for Varn, he wanted out.

"There it is!" shouted Mertane. He was pointing to a dark fixed shop at the back corner of the markets. It was an ominous looking shop which blended into its surroundings. Varn thought it looked plain and unimportant, but he didn't care, he was relieved. "That is where we will find all the answers to help save the princess from certain death."

Chapter Twelve

"Ouch!" she cried, "ouch!" she cried again.

"Oh do stop complaining, it's like you've never had your eyebrows plucked into shape before," retorted Lady Jane, "and by the state in which you've presented this morning I wouldn't be surprised."

"I've never felt such pain," explained Mary, "If this is what you call beautification then I'd be happy being ugly."

"Oh do stop," commanded Lady Jane. And with that Mary stopped complaining, although Lady Jane did try not to be as vigorous with her eyebrow line and only concentrated on the stray, unkempt hairs.

Lit torches on the wall behind Lady Jane illuminated Mary's face as she sat before her. Although at times she was in pain, Mary was loving every moment of her treatment. She had never felt this much attention from anyone, well Samuel of course but he was a cat. She tried to keep her head straight and forward, as she was always reminded, but she couldn't help her eyes from darting at every new instrument or method being applied to her body. Whether it was her toe nails being trimmed, her leg hairs being removed - this was the most painful - or her cheeks being flush with crimson paste. She loved it all.

She had had a warm bath in steaming hot, clean water. She was scrubbed by a firm bristled brush on a long wooden handle. Slippery white blocks called soap were used on her and she grinned in awe as the clean water turned murky over time.

Now Mary stood in the center of the room on top of a small ornate box with cushion padding fixed to the top with gold studs. Although she was dressed in a drab, off-white undergarment, which wasn't really shapely, she still felt cold. She hated being the center of attention at the center of the room.

"Your dress is almost here," explained Lady Jane. "Poor thing, you must be nervous, but the wait will be quite worth it."

"May I ask you one question, please, Miss Lady Jane?"

"Of course," answered Lady Jane, with a slight quiver in her voice as she was fearful of where this question was going to lead.

"Why?" asked Mary. She stood there with sullen expression, looking into Lady Jane's eyes for an answer as to why she was here, why now, why all the attention.

"Why, what?" replied Lady Jane, knowing quite well what she was truly asking but hoping it was something trivial. Lady Jane was beginning to sense and realize that Mary was not an ordinary prisoner, that Mary was quite different, more aware. In fact Mary seemed to be behaving and communicating as though she was one of the best educated in the kingdom. She was starting to show care for her, even though the princess she served would have had her executed for even the thought of such a thing.

"Why me, why remove me from prison, a place where I know no different, strip me bare and then clean and treat me like a..." she paused trying to think of the right words. "...treat me like royalty?"

The relationship that existed between Mary and Princess Margaret was unknown to Lady Jane. It was unknown to almost everyone. Because of Mary's lifelong treatment by Princess Margaret she was concerned why all of a sudden her fortune seemed to change. Lady Jane was also dumbfounded and was perplexed as to why Mary's life suddenly stood on end but she knew what fate lay ahead for her. She chose her words wisely so she didn't reveal her fate, otherwise Lady Jane knew it would be her alongside Mary for tonight's celebrations.

"Tonight you are a special guest and I have been personally requested by the princess to prepare you and present you in celebration attire," explained Lady Jane, wincing inside and relieved she didn't have to make eye contact with Mary as she finished braiding her hair.

"To what celebration? er Miss Lady Jane?" asked Mary.

"Didn't you hear the bells ringing yesterday?"

"Bells?" questioned Mary "I am afraid I didn't." Mary slept during the day and this was due to her malnutrition and weakness. So she was most likely asleep while the bells chimed. She probably combined them into a dream and couldn't separate them from reality.

"Thirteen chimes at noon signify the death of royalty," Lady Jane explained, "the king has passed away."

Tears started to welt under Mary's eyes as she realized what Lady Jane was saying.

"Princess Margaret wants to become queen, but in order to do so she must hold the funeral for the king and celebrate his life with a banquet, and you are invited to this banquet."

"I am more than just a banquet guest aren't I Miss Lady Jane?" asked Mary, frankly and direct.

Before Lady Jane could find the strength to answer her they both spun around quickly and stared at the doorway. Their mouths dropped to the sight of a black cat, leaning up against the architrave staring back at them, with a blue orb amulet dangling from its collar. What was most striking though was that the amulet was glowing.

Chapter Thirteen

Varn followed Mertane as he pushed through thick leather curtains that hung in the shop entrance. To the right side of them their eyes were instantly drawn to the hulk of a figure who was forging steel with an iron hammer. The steel was still glowing red from the nearby fire and the clinking and banging made Varn blink with each strike. The glow of the fire radiated across the blacksmith's glistening chest as he fashioned the steel uncaring for the new customers that entered the store.

Varn didn't know where to look. Farming tools flanked the walls to the left of them and in front of them to the back of the store there were religious crosses and adornments. Like what you would decorate a church with or more likely frame a gravesite with.

On tables in front of the blacksmith there were leather wares like coats and warrior's chaps. Racks and racks of stretched cow and goat hides of many different colours and sizes were stacked in one corner and in the other were saddles and bridles and other dressage equipment. Varn was in awe of the craftsmanship of the leather wrapped shields and metal swords that stood proudly at the center of the room. Mertane gave him a quick tap on the back of the hand to stop it wandering and getting into trouble as it reached for a longing touch of the stunning weapons.

"Um, excuse me sir," Mertane gestured towards the blacksmith. He wasn't listening, couldn't hear or simply ignored Mertane, so Mertane approached a little closer.

"Excuse me sir, can I please have some of your precious time?" he continued. The blacksmith seemed to strike harder on the iron, sparks flew up from each blow. He seemed to be creating a sickle, its sharp edge being formed in front of the two unwelcome strangers.

"Just a couple of very important questions? You would be a savior to our kingdom, would you not?" pushed Mertane. This time he must have struck a chord with the blacksmith, but Mertane got a response he wasn't expecting. The blacksmith caught both Mertane and Varn of guard as he lashed out forward with the glowing red sickle and forging hammer. They both fell back and knocked over a rack of forged stew pots. They were both quite vulnerable and thought they were finished at the mercy of the blacksmith, cut up and pulverized at the hands of a hulking beast. With eyes firmly closed and hands raised to protect themselves they winced and waited.

"He won't answer you, you know," said a quiet and scratchy voice.

Mertane and Varn slowly lowered their arms and simultaneously turned their heads to peer at who spoke to them. She looked like a frail old woman in her twilight years. Her hair was grey and thin, it framed her yellowing face like unkempt vines around an ancient forest temple. She was quite short and both men didn't need to stand to make level eye contact with her but they did out of respect and bowed their heads. "Pardon me madam, we don't mean to cause any trouble," Mertane apologized.

She studied them with squinting eyes for a small moment. She didn't recognize them but she could see they were no threat to her especially with Saxon there to protect her. Before Mertane and Varn could work out what she was thinking she turned abruptly and said, "follow me, we must leave Saxon alone."

They followed the old lady carefully and cautiously as they heard Saxon continue to hammer away on the sickle. This whole encounter was all a bit too much for Varn and he let Mertane take the lead, almost hiding behind his cloak. She led them to the back of the store to a large rough sawn bench to where the sales took place. From behind the counter she sat up on a raised stool with much gusto and stared down her irritants. "Now, who are you and what do you want?"

"I am Mertane and my apprentice is Varn, we've come from His Majesty's Castle. We were hoping that you'd recognize this?" explained Mertane and without pause he took off the blue glowing amulet from around his neck and placed it on the counter. He cleverly omitted the fact that he was the Master Wizard of Kingsgate as he didn't want to scare Beatrice with his potential sorcery.

"I saw it around your scrawny neck the minute you entered my shop, hell I even felt its presence when you both rode into Shadow Valley," she spat. "You wear it and yet you don't know what it's for?" she asked, coughing slightly and eyeing Mertane with a suspicious look. This time she paused for what seemed like an eternity before she questioned Mertane with both her arms raised, "does this look like a charity to you?"

"Of course not, you will be compensated for your knowledge," reasoned Mertane.

"Good, good," she said as she rolled her thick tongue over her lips.

"Look," he said, "I know the story behind the amulet, why the amulet is here, it's a protection charm for the kingdom, is it not madam?"

"You may call me Beatrice not madam, and yes that is correct, it is a protection amulet," she spat at them crankily.

"My apologies Beatrice, I had a feeling that I had come to the right place for answers. Thank God you are here and can help," explained Mertane. "As I've explained, I know what the amulet is for, but I am unsure why it has started to glow and why it's getting brighter?"

A large cockroach scuttled from under a pile of leather sheets draped over the counter beside her right arm. It stopped intermittently checking for things it could eat as it crawled along, towards the edge of the wooden counter, with its antenna flailing about. Without taking her eyes off Mertane, Beatrice picked up a leather riding glove that she had been mending, before she was interrupted, and slammed it down hard on the insect. It cracked with a snap and yellow guts flicked across Mertane's cloak. Some got on Varn's face which he promptly wiped off.

"I hope I am not being too rude as to hasten you along, please Mrs Beatrice. We don't have much time," pleaded Mertane.

"It's Beatrice to you, not Mrs Beatrice. I was never a Mrs and I never will be. No man, king or wizard will ever rule me," she said sternly.

"Yes Beatrice, please go on."

"The amulet you wear is one in a set of three. Each would be glowing now, all at the same time." she explained. As she did it seemed she mellowed a little. It was like she was relieving herself of an emotional burden that she had harbored for many years. "The reason they are glowing is that King Henry has died," she said bluntly.

"What do you mean died, that cannot be," said Mertane as both he and Varn looked at each other in shock. Mertane had just been grappling with the idea that there were three amulets, but the news of the death of his good friend King Henry floored him and sent a hot flush over his body and a heavy knot in his stomach. "But, but," he stuttered, "but I was just explaining to Varn before we came to Shadow Valley that the amulet had once glowed many years ago. King Henry had given it to me then to look after and said the glow will one day extinguish, which it did, he can't be dead!"

"Unfortunately he is and so too the death of the protection spell was inevitable," she stated, unemotional. The original protection spell was born within the amulet, it was bright to begin with but its strength slowly petered out in forever diminishing loops," explained Beatrice.

"Precisely!" exclaimed Mertane. "So when the amulet started glowing again I assumed that the protection spell was rejuvenating."

"Wrong," said Beatrice bluntly. "When King Henry, the late King Henry, had taken the amulets from a neighboring kingdom, Brookhaven, during unrest. He had the wizard of Brookhaven at the time activate them to protect his family, little did he know that there was also a curse placed on them at the same time."

"Extraordinary!" said Mertane. He was gobsmacked.

"The curse was a safety net put in place by the wizard. He hated seeing the kingdom he had served all his life being taken away, even though it wasn't King Henry's fault. He was merely protecting himself from its evil ruler, King Charles. It was conquer or be conquered."

"Yes, right," ushered Mertane.

"The curse was ultimately placed on all that was held dear to King Henry. His wife, Queen Margaret the First died of a mysterious illness not long after the kingdom was taken if you remember," explained Beatrice. "Once the king has died the curse would be broken."

Varn was beginning to become more nervous as he heard Saxon stop fashioning the steel. He was also out of sight, as the flames of his fire pit were illuminating the corner of the shop.

"King Henry had told me in confidence many years ago that if he died a force so great would place his kin in danger," said Mertane, "but from what you are telling me is that once the curse is lifted then all should be well?"

"You have no understanding of the true power of the amulet, the nature of the curse and the way in which the curse will die," spat Beatrice. "You bumble in here like lambs with no shepherd."

"As you say," retorted Mertane annoyed at Beatrice's friction.

"Do you know what happens to a stray lamb out here on the plains of Shadow Valley?" poked Beatrice.

"One could only imagine."

"Yes one could, but I'll tell you exactly. The wolf gets a full belly, is what happens," stabs Beatrice. Her dialogue was wandering from the final answers Mertane was needing. He too was becoming nervous. They had been here far too long. Precious time was wasting.

"Please Beatrice, what danger did King Henry warn me of, and how is it that Princess Margaret was unscathed by the curse."

"Payment is what I need, now Wizard Mertane, I've said too much," and with that Beatrice parted a leather curtain behind her which led to a back room. "SAXON!" she screamed, "I need you to pound money from these two lambs before you eat them!"

Chapter Fourteen

"Where are those useless dressmakers!" screeched Princess Margaret. "If I have to wait one moment longer then heads will roll." Princess Margaret was standing in the middle of her royal chambers, beside her late father's bed which was now hers. She was wearing a black lace undergarment, as advised by the stylists, to be the best match for the dress she was about to wear. She had her servants fussing over her getting her ready for tonight's important proceedings. There were hairdressers shaping her long black hair into an amazing plated sculpture, trimming, shaving and pinning her hair. There were beauticians decorating her face with thick yet pronounced make up. There were dress fitters nervously darting their heads back and forth looking concerned towards Princess Margaret and then scowling at the door. Other dress fitters and servants were hovering around the doorway looking down the hallway and shrugging back towards those who orbited around Princess Margaret.

"It shan't be too long your excellency," one of the stylists nervously said.

"It better not be!" retorted Princess Margaret. "Or one by one I'll personally push you out that window," she said pointing to one of her floor to ceiling windows.

Just before the pressure got too much and the servants themselves jumped out that window noises were heard from outside, down the hallway. Heaving and scraping, huffing and puffing.

"Good," said Princess Margaret as she too heard the noise and assumed it was her dress being delivered.

Four muscular men wearing only leather trousers with suspenders and beads of sweat dripping from their bare chests each helped carry in a large wooden box. The box was sitting on two large timber beams and each man carried one end of a beam. They ambled the box to the side of the room and each groaned as they lowered it to the floor.

Thump.

The men then proceeded to lift the timber box up and over a frame that was attached to the timber beams. There at the center of the frame, on a dress form, was the most magnificent dress that was ever made in the kingdom. It was elegant, it was beautiful, even Princess Margaret had to control herself, she didn't want to look too joyous. Not yet anyway, this dress had to fit.

The dress was made entirely from large loops of gold chain. It had chains draped over the shoulder in a Queen-Anne style, then they all came together at the waist, which flowed outwards in a ball gown fashion. Pink diamonds shimmered at the waist and radiated downwards in long strings. The chains and diamond combination looked like fireworks petering out before coming back to earth. Just stunning.

Two of the men lifted the dress off the form slowly and gently, trying not to damage the gold chains or get them caught. Even though the strong men looked like they were struggling with the weight of the dress the princess couldn't wait for them to place it on her. They side stepped over, towards Princess Margaret, and under the careful guide of the dress fitters and seamstresses. With her welcoming nod the dress was lifted high above her head and slowly lowered over her body. Princess Margaret kept her arms out so she could slip them under the shoulder bands. Ever so slowly the men released the weight of the dress.

Princess Margaret turned in her new dress, she faced a mirror which was temporarily set up beside her. She wavered slightly and the dressmakers gasped. She shimmered in the daylight. She almost got herself into position to inspect herself in the mirror when one of her legs gave way to the weight of the dress and she crashed to the floor. She landed on her side and she winced in pain. Staff dropped just as quickly as she did in order to assist her. "Whoever made this wretched dress so heavy will spend eternity in the dungeon!" she screamed.

Chapter Fifteen

"Samuel!" cried Mary. She thought that he surely had been killed by the guards. "You're alive!" she wailed as she jumped off the box and ran over to him, scooping him up in one motion. She squeezed and hugged him, spinning around in circles as though she was waltzing with him. He purred and rubbed his head against her vigorously.

"Is he yours?" asked Lady Jane. She was more perplexed with the glowing amulet around his neck. She had never seen such a thing before.

"Yes, yes, yes," cried Mary. "He's mine, his name is Samuel and he's all I have." Mary returned to the center of the room and sat down on the box. She placed Samuel on her lap and began to stroke him as he continued purring. "That's different, Samuel. Your neck charm is glowing, I wonder why?" Mary dismissed the amulet's appearance for now as she was more overjoyed for being reunited with Samuel. "Miss Lady Jane, can Samuel be looked after please while I am at the dinner?"

"Yes of course, we can make sure he is safe upon your return," she lied. "Now, let me see what is keeping those dressmakers," she said as she quickly exited the room feeling guilty.

Mary turned to Samuel and gave him a good scratch under his chin. "Samuel, I've missed you so much," she said to him soothingly as he purred, "you must stay out of trouble, I fear we are both in grave danger, except I don't know what is going to happen."

Samuel jumped down off of Mary's lap and slinked out a few meters in front of Mary. He quickly sat down, extended a hind leg out and started licking it profusely. "Well I know I am getting cleaned up," Mary stated, "so I suppose you should clean yourself as well." He turned his head to look back at Mary and gave her a squinting look, "Yes, yes, I know you wouldn't like anyone else cleaning you except yourself." It was like Samuel knew she was talking about him and he turned around and jumped back on Mary's lap. "Come back for another scratch, have you?" she asked. "Just promise me one thing that no matter what happens, you never leave me again."

Just then Lady Jane pushed her way through the doorway carrying a large crate, she was closely followed by two other women. "Your dress is ready," she said, "and these seamstresses will help fit it on you and make any necessary adjustments."

"Thank you so very much," said Mary as she rose and stood back up on the box at the center of the room. Samuel groaned as his petting session promptly stopped and he was put back on the floor. He raced over to the corner of the room, turned around and sat down. Sitting in the shadows he felt safe from all the fussing about and the new people in the room, but still kept a keen eye on Mary.

"I have other business to attend to, you will be looked after by these two lovely ladies and they will inform me when they are done," instructed Lady Jane. Mary looked at Lady Jane timidly with a hint of fear in her eyes. "Don't worry Mary, although the guard is still present outside the room you will still be safe in here," she said comfortingly. "I'll be back when you are done to escort you to the Grand Dining Hall." With that she turned and left the room. Mary heard voices out in the hallway, she thought it may have been Lady Jane giving the guard stern instructions. She hoped so.

One of the seamstresses pulled the dress from out of the crate which was on the floor. She held it up from the shoulder straps in front of her and let it unfurl to its full length. 'Wow,' thought Mary. She hadn't seen anything so beautiful in her whole life. The dress was a simple body hugging form, its fabric was ivory coloured with lace inlay and sewn glass beads in a floral pattern. It would have taken weeks to create. Without hesitation both the seamstresses pulled the dress over Mary's head and started to tug and pull to arrange it into position. They then pulled and fussed about the fabric ensuring that they captured any ill-fitting sections. "Pretty good for a first fitting," one of them said proudly of themselves. One of them gathered a couple of sections of fabric at Mary's flank, pulled it tight together and pinned it in place. "There," said the seamstress, "this is all the adjustment we need."

"Thank you," said Mary as the dress was lifted back over her head and returned to the crate. She was left cold again in her under garment. Both the seamstresses curtseyed to Mary before they left the room with the dress to make the final alterations. Mary felt a sudden rush of discomfort, she was slightly embarrassed, she had never been curtseyed to before.

Mary sat back down on the box that she had been standing on for her dress fitting. The coast was clear for Samuel so he slinked from the shadows and jumped back up on her lap. He gave a loud meow in appreciation as Mary started giving him his much loved chin and neck scratch. "It shouldn't be too long, Samuel, before Miss Lady Jane returns," she said as she gazed at him.

Suddenly they both heard voices from the hallway outside, they turned their heads as the doorway curtain was drawn and a woman wearing a black suit burst into the room and presented herself in a commanding position. "So that is your rat!" screeched Princess Margaret.

Chapter Sixteen

Saxon burst through the curtains in rage, nearly tearing them off the rods from which they hung. He didn't waste any time and threw himself across the counter launching himself with both arms out ready to grab Mertane and Varn in one swoop. Both visitors managed to just step aside to miss his grasp. Saxon fell to the floor, empty handed, which enraged him even more, "Aaaaahh," he screamed.

Varn looked at Mertane wide eyed in shock and fear. How would they get out of this situation unscathed? Beatrice stood behind the counter, smirking as she watched the show. This was exciting for her. Mertane had no time to react, Saxon had targeted him and was now bearing down on him. In what appeared to be quite a flexible move for such a large hulk of a man, Saxon now sprung up and threw himself at Mertane. This time he had a decent handful of Mertane's cloak. Varn gulped and grimaced anticipating the blow.

With one hand holding his captor, Saxon swung a closed fist around like he was swinging an axe into the side of a tree. There was a dull thud as his fist met a thick cloak. But that was all it was. Now Saxon's rage quickly turned to surprise as he gave Beatrice a bewildered look. All that Saxon held was Mertane's empty cloak.

"You hoo," taunted Mertane from behind a pile of leather at the other side of the room.

Saxon saw red, his blood boiled and he ran screaming towards Mertane. He didn't appreciate the party trick. "Oh no," cried Varn. He was sure this would be the end of his master.

Mertane began to chant with his arms held apart in front of him and with his fingers spread apart pointing toward each other as though he was holding an invisible ball. His chants grew louder as Saxon came closer. Suddenly a burst of light appeared between Mertane's hands, Saxon was still charging strongly and was dangerously close to his target.

Boom! The light cracked and illuminated the whole shop. Saxon was thrown backwards but froze midair. Beatrice's face drew fear, but she also couldn't move. The light between Mertane's fingers now withdrew from its long vertical lightning bolt shape into a more spherical orb. Mertane was able to move the light orb around and he placed it in between Saxon and

Beatrice, part way off the floor. Varn was in awe as the levitating orb shone streams of light around the room and flickered shadows on all their faces.

"Now, Beatrice, where were we? Ah yes, what of the dangers of the Amulet and please explain Princess Margaret's doing in all of this?" demanded Mertane in a stern voice. He was well and truly over the shenanigans that had gone on.

Beatrice couldn't budge. She had been under this spell before, but this time it was much stronger. She feared what might come next shouldn't she oblige. "Yes, you are a strong wizard, Sir Mertane, and wise to have kept that secret from me until now" she started. "I am quite amazed that you hadn't found out the truth of the amulet sooner, since you have one hanging around your neck."

Mertane glared at Beatrice. "Okay, okay, the truth you seek, the truth you shall get," squirmed Beatrice. "The power of the amulet is great, King Henry knew it as he saw its power first hand. You would think that when King Henry died that the curse would be lifted and his precious daughter would be safe. But no, the King knew it would only be the start. Yes his wife had died from the curse, but the wizard who placed the curse, Master Wizard Jotane, created the curse with a final cleansing element. He wanted all that were responsible for his life being upturned to be themselves upturned. The glowing amulets are simply the true beginning of the end."

Mertane's mind raced as Beatrice spat out all that she knew. Varn thought it was quite funny watching her talk. Her body and head were frozen into position and all that moved were her darting eyes and her mouth going up and down. "What about

Princess Margaret, what danger is she in?" Varn questioned, his head was spinning too. If she could turn her head and glare at Varn she would. 'How rude, how unbelievably insolent to interject,' she thought. Normally she wouldn't give a child the time of day, but she knew she was in an unfortunate predicament.

"Princess Margaret was part of Jotane's bigger plan. Yes she is in grave danger now as she will become the next ruler of Kingsgate, her power will be too great and inevitably she will pay the ultimate price," she explained.

"How do we stop this force, the final act of this curse?" Mertane asked sternly.

"All I know," said Beatrice poignantly, "is that all three amulets need to be brought together by the last three surviving royalty." Her eyes began to burn, her body was not boding well under this spell. She needed to rest and her voice was losing its strength. "Then the curse will be undone."

Mertane and Varn stared at each other in disbelief. Three royalty, how could this be true. As far as Mertane knew Princess Margaret was now the only living royalty left in Kingsgate. "Please, just finally before I let you go Beatrice," he could see he would have to end the spell soon, before it was too late, "I only know of Princess Margaret and you speak of two more royalty?"

"And I only know of a second child that King Henry bore, she grew up here in Shadow Valley, on the outskirts, raised by maize farmers under the name of Mary," Beatrice's eyes grew heavy now and if her head could it would have slumped forward.

"Forgive my ignorance Beatrice, but how do I know all this is true? You seem to know quite a bit for being an old lady in a sleepy town, and it all seems a bit far-fetched," questioned

Mertane as he turned his head, checking to see if Saxon was still contained and he too wasn't close to death under the holding spell.

"Believe what you will Master Wizard Mertane," she said as a tear rolled down her cheek, "but before our kingdom was invaded, before Master Wizard Jotane was captured and imprisoned he was to be married," she hesitated once more, " he was to be my husband." Beatrice blacked out.

Chapter Seventeen

Her black dress, which was full length, absorbed the shadows as she walked over to Mary. The thick pleated bodice flowed out from the tight waist like feathers on an ostriches back. Even her arms were covered in black fabric, cascading down her arms from high shoulder ruffles, giving her a masculine presence. Her black shiny hair was plated in many individual strands and looped above her head in the shape of a bird cage.

With her head bowed towards the floor, Mary's eye nervously looked up. Without control and by mistake she sniggered at

Princess Margaret's hair style. Just as quickly as she contained her emotion Princess Margaret's hand swung down and across her body wildly. Mary was shocked that it connected with her face and sent a searing pain across her mouth as her head was knocked sideways by the blow. Samuel hissed and ran out the door making a wide berth past Princess Margaret and running between the legs of the guards as they clumsily bent down to grab him, but missing him.

"How disrespectful," Princess Margaret screamed. "The prisoner must stand!" As Mary stood she felt blood start to drip from the corner of her mouth. The pain was unbearable, but she refused to cry and held back the tears as her eyes welted up.

"Yes, your majesty," Mary said sarcastically, standing tall, proud and full of resolve, not caring what punishment might come next.

Princess Margaret scowled and moved uncomfortably close to Mary. There was an even more uncomfortable pause as Princess Margaret stared into Mary's eyes. It was like a domination ploy on who would look away first. Neither did. "If you haven't worked it out by now, tonight is very special for me," she began, as she spoke she began to walk around Mary and made her way back to face her, "and by this small display of insubordination I am worried that you will ruin my moment."

"Please, your majesty, I won't," pleaded Mary, with her head bowed and looking towards the floor. Her blood was dry now but her cheek was marked by a red flush. Maybe it would bruise.

"Silence!" screamed Princess Margaret. "The prisoner won't speak unless it is asked." As she barked the order Mary flinched with every spittle that landed on her face.

"If you upset tonight's proceedings then we will hunt down that cat of yours and it will be..., let's just say that would have been the last time you saw it alive." threatened Princess Margaret. Tears now began to welt in Mary's eye, she'd learnt to contain her emotions quite well in her life due to her harsh upbringing and all the life's lessons that it had brought but when it came to Samuel she couldn't control them.

"Now, now," coaxed Princess Margaret in a taunting and condescending way, "you have nothing to worry about, that rat of yours will be safe. That is, if you don't upset the night." She paced around Mary again.

Just then a burly guard entered the room, "Er, excuse me your highness."

"What is it, it better be good news," said Princess Margaret.

"Yes your majesty, the cat is captured," he stated with a blank stare. Mary's body tensed and she lifted her head up to look at Princess Margaret directly.

"Good, good," said the princess, noticing Mary's change in demeanor, "make sure it's cooked before you feed it to the royal dogs, I don't want them having upset stomachs, it will ruin the royal lawns."

"No!" screamed Mary.

"More insubordination," screamed the princess, and with that she grabbed Mary's throat with both hands. The sudden attack took Mary off her feet, but she didn't topple over as she was too close to the wall and was pinned back to it with a thud. Now Princess Margaret had her face almost up against Mary's. Mary braced herself against the wall with her free hands. "This is what I am talking about, any further challenges and I will go through with my instructions to the guard" she kept screaming into Mary's face all the while her grip around her throat tightened. Mary started to go red, her eyes felt like they were popping from her skull, and her breath was escaping her. She was starting to choke, "do you understand?" screamed Princess Margaret again. She couldn't breathe let alone talk, so she tried to nod. Princess Margaret saw the response and threw Mary to the ground.

"Oh and if you do make me unhappy tonight, I wouldn't worry about what would happen to your cat, no I'd worry about what would happen to you." Just then Lady Jane ran into the room, she looked down at Mary in concern and then up towards Princess Margaret.

Princess Margaret walked towards the door of the room, she was done, she was leaving. Without hesitation and regard to acknowledging Lady Jane she said, "make sure you cover those bruises on her neck, I don't want that to be what the people focus on before I hang my sister."

Chapter Eighteen

"One last stop before we get back to the castle, son," Mertane explained as they galloped on their horse, heading out of Shadow Valley. Mertane had made sure he left Beatrice and Saxon in good order, although they would be sleeping for a couple of days to recover. Their shop would be protected under a security spell and they would have little recollection, although a few stiff joints and bruises, of what had transpired.

"Where are we going, it's going to be too late to save Princess Margaret," pleaded Varn. He was struggling to hold onto Mertane.

"We have to visit the only maize farm in Shadow Valley, we need to find the rest of this royal family," he explained, "there's no use turning up to a 'fight' without all our 'weapons', we'd be doomed otherwise."

They made their way past rolling fields separated by fencing and stocked each with cattle, dairy cows and sheep. These fields soon gave way to fields of crops like wheat, barley and finally maize. Maize was a staple crop that was milled into flour for addition into bread and also given raw to the dairy cows for food supplement. It was an easy crop to grow, it was a safe choice for the king to pick maize farmers. There was no risk of being trampled by livestock at a young age, there was less risk of being targeted by farm looters.

Mertane turned off the dirt road and headed down the grass track which led to the farm house. It was quite a vast farm, the farmhouse was quite a distance off the main road. All that could be seen up ahead over the top of the maize fields was a plume of smoke, most likely from a kitchen chimney.

As they got closer the maize fields parted to a clearing and in the middle of a small rise a timber house stood quaintly. At the base of the small rise was a large granite stone wheel with a circular track for a mule to draw the wheel around on a frame. 'Most likely for crushing the maize into flour,' thought Varn.

Mertane and Varn dismounted and quickly spun their heads around as the farmhouse door creaked open and a middle aged man peaked through with his wife following closely and nervously behind him. "State your name and business," he yelled.

"Please, please, we come as your friend, we mean you no harm and we do apologize for this unsolicited visit," Mertane explained, "I, Mertane and my young apprentice Varn, are seeking some answers that you may know."

Suddenly the farmer's wife pushed past her husband and she ran down the embankment crying profusely. Her husband ran to catch up with her. "What is it woman, please be careful, we don't know these folk," he pleaded, trying to drag her back by her long sleeved blouse.

"Can't you see it Thomas," she cried, "it's our boy, it's William!"

"I must apologize," said Thomas, "our boy went missing many years ago and both Elizabeth and I were devastated." As the sun began to set a long shadow was cast across the valley. The temperature dropped quickly and Mertane felt a chill.

"Can we please talk inside, we have some important questions to ask, even if you believe Varn here is your son," asked Mertane. They were ushered quickly inside as Varn's cheeks went crimson with embarrassment by the attention Elizabeth was giving him. She wouldn't let him go.

Once inside the guests took off their heavy cloaks and were directed to sit at a small round table. Elizabeth filled tea cups, which were tarnished and chipped, with a hot liquid from a copper teapot. The teapot had been warming by hanging from a wrought iron frame within the fireplace hearth. "Drink up, it's a warm herbal tea," she insisted. Mertane reluctantly sipped the liquid and grimaced, herbal wasn't his favorite brew, but the tea did warm him up. "How can Varn be your son?" he began, "Varn is my nephew and I've known him since he was a boy."

"How old was he exactly, you only knew him from when he was a boy, not a baby?" asked Elizabeth, wary of Mertane's true knowledge of his 'nephews' origins.

"It's true, I didn't first see Varn until he was two or so, but that was because my sister was from out of town, she wouldn't lie to me, Varn is of my blood," explained Mertane.

Thomas and Elizabeth looked at each other, and she ran and buried her head into Thomas' chest crying uncontrollably. "Mertane, our boy was taken from us when he was two, he was playing out in the front. It was a beautiful day. But it is a day we will never forget.

"Even so, how do you know this young sixteen year old boy was your two year old son?" questioned Mertane.

Elizabeth stopped sobbing, she came over to Varn, who didn't know where to look, but now was captivated by her stare. She knelt down beside him and looked into his eyes, "his eyes are still as beautiful as they were then as they are today. I can tell, a mother never forgets her child's eyes. I stared for hours upon hours, gazing into his eyes. He was a beautiful baby."

"Okay, but I need some hard evidence, this is just not enough for me," pleaded Mertane, he was beginning to get a headache.

Elizabeth looked up at Thomas then back towards Varn, "If you are truly our William then on the back of your right shoulder are three small moles in a line, they are perfectly up and down." Varn stood up instantly, his chair toppled over behind him from his sudden movement. Mertane rose as well, stood behind Varn and pulled his shirt down from his collar exposing his right shoulder blade. There in the warm light of the glowing fireplace were three moles one above the other, straight up and down in a perfect line.

"What a day!" Mertane exhaled. He was emotionally exhausted, "and here I was coming to ask if you had a daughter of royal blood."

Elizabeth and Thomas both looked at each other in bewilderment again. This time Thomas spoke as Elizabeth was inconsolable as she wept holding her William. "You see Mertane, now that we know this is William, we've never told anyone this but William did have a twin sister, we lost her when she wandered into the maize fields when she was six."

"We were trying hard for a child," Elizabeth said sobbing and staring at Mertane through tear filled eyes, "but I was barren and we couldn't conceive." She looked at Thomas now and smiled, her thoughts brought her back to the very day that her life changed. "We were so grateful that someone left these two beautiful babies at our doorstep. They were wrapped up snuggly. They were perfect."

"Extraordinary!" exclaimed Mertane as he scratched his beard in disbelief.

"We've been shell shocked ever since William was taken," Thomas continued on for Elizabeth who was still miles away in thought about that day she will never forget, "and we've never recovered since we lost our beautiful Mary."

Chapter Nineteen

"Fellow royalty, honorary distinguished guests, stately friends of the throne, servants and civics, warriors and workers, ladies and gentlemen, please be upstanding in joining me to welcome your future queen, Princess Margaret," announced Lord James.

The guests who were stirring now stood erect and were captivated by the commanding voice of Lord James. His presence was respected and admired, he held the crowd's attention and was why he was the best choice for chairman of this evening's and tonight's proceedings. He was Master of Ceremony.

Trumpets played and filled the halls of the chamber with striking resonance. Together with the deep base of the drums and the brassy trumpet tones the music was felt in the chests of all. It truly was an uplifting moment.

Everyone was facing forwards except for Lord James and the entourage that were standing behind the pulpit looking towards the back of the castle chapel. To his right was the kingdom's head priest flanked by his clergy and assistants. Suddenly heads turned as the large oak entrance doors at the back of the chapel opened with a cracking sound. The noise was caused because the doors 'stuck' to each other due to their immense weight when they were closed. It was like breaking a timber seal and it took a lot of effort to open them. Because of this they were rarely closed and only shut this evening for a dramatic entrance.

The drums stopped beating as trumpets began to play an uplifting tune. In single file entered the royal procession, Princess Margaret, followed by assistants then Lady Jane followed by her assistants, a nervous Mary and finally a handful of guards. All were dressed in black except for Mary who still wore her undergarments that she had on in the dressmaking chamber. Lady Jane had objected to this but it was a stern order from Princess Margaret. "The prisoner will show respect, it shall be known she is a prisoner, she is not one of us!" she had spat at poor Lady Jane. There was appropriate funeral attire made for Mary, but they weren't to be worn today.

The music wound down and silence was heard across the hall, all except the occasional cough as the royalty made their way to the left of Lord James and sat in their respective seats. "Before we move on to proceedings of grandeur, before we appoint the new queen, let us take a moment to reflect upon, to properly farewell and to pay our respects to our late heroic leader, King Henry." Cheers erupted around the cavernous walls of the castle's chapel. Lord James who was standing behind the pulpit now turned to his side. He gulped as his glance caught Princess Margaret glaring at him. Sitting beside her was Lady Jane and to her side was Mary. He couldn't help but notice her nervousness and the chain around her ankle, presumably the other end was secured by the guard standing behind her.

Lord James turned back to the mourners. "Please, please, quiet please," he boomed motioning his hands downward to quieten the hubbub. As the noise died down he continued, "I shall now hand over proceedings to Priest John who will respectfully reflect upon King Henry's rule, his life and his people." Lord James took his seat beside Princess Margaret who didn't look at him but kept her stare forward.

Suddenly trumpets blared out a tune in quick succession then stopped abruptly. There was a short silence and then a harp was played in the music quarters of the chapel accompanied by the harrowing voice of a female singer who sang a traditional Celtic hymn. The singing continued as two rows of six pallbearers carried King Henry's coffin down the center aisle of the chapel and placed it on a large stone plinth at the foot of the pulpit. The music was beautiful, it danced around the large chapel like a butterfly flitting over a bramble grove in flower.

And so the funeral took place. There were readings from the bible, long religious rhetoric which tried to bring assimilation to life and death and King Henry's role in society. There was singing and even an awkward performance from the castle jester. Finally when Priest John closed the ceremony with the Lord's Prayer he asked for the mourners to pay their respects and lay a wreath or flower on King Henry's coffin. First to do so however was the royal party.

Princess Margaret stood first and took a single crimson rose with rich blood red tips of the petals from a basket of flowers. She placed it on top of the coffin, she took a moment, perhaps to reflect on her father's life, perhaps it was a staged show of emotion, before she left with her assistants in tow and a couple of guards out a side entrance at the head of the chapel.

Mary touched her throat gingerly and winced at its tenderness. "Come," said Lady Jane, noticing her pain. They both stood and approached the coffin. Lady Jane placed a rose on the coffin and turned to Mary, giving her a nod of approval and standing back from her, giving her room. She didn't let Mary out of her sight and made sure the guard who was holding the chain didn't make any inhumane moves. Lady Jane nodded and motioned her hand as to say, 'go on', when Mary turned back to look at her again. Mary's quivering hand reached out and picked up a red rose. It was one of the most beautiful things she had ever touched. She couldn't remember the last time she held a rose, but she thought she must have done it before, it felt familiar.

Mary gently placed the rose on top of the large wooden coffin. It had been meticulously crafted from cherry red oak, the king's favorite timber, hand carved with ornate and intricate scenes throughout history and finally hand polished to a mirror finish. Beads of water from the freshly cut roses dotted the top of the coffin beside the flowers. It looked like tears.

Her eyes began to welt as she thought of the lost opportunity of ever meeting her father, without ever spending time with him. She searched her mind for a memory with him but it came up blank. Her earliest memory was of playing in a grassy meadow with a black kitten, Samuel. From then on it was like her memories were erased because all she could remember was being locked up. Tears gently streamed down her cheeks. They weren't tears of sorrow or despair, but tears of anger. Why was she being paraded around like this, what had she done to deserve it. Why wasn't she afforded the freedom of a normal life?

Lady Jane came over and held Mary at the shoulders to comfort her. "Come, Mary," she whispered, "I will find a way to free you before it's too late." Mary looked up at her with hope in her eyes. She wiped the tears from her face and studied Lady Jane. She whispered to Mary in a caring and nurturing manner, almost like mother to daughter. "Sweet Mary, please forgive me," she continued also now with tears streaming down her face, staring blankly at the coffin, "the last time the three of us were all together as a family was shortly after I gave birth to you."

Chapter Twenty

Flames from rows of torches mounted on marble columns flickered and cast dancing shadows across the palace patio and out into the gardens. The torches which lined the courtyard stood like tall soldiers guarding the perimeter of the vast courtyard. This was to be the venue for the coronation of the queen. The outdoor area was agreed upon by the princess because it had enough space for all the kingdom's people but mainly because it was the only area large enough to quickly erect and house a hanging stage.

The stage was fabricated on the side of the courtyard. It looked out of place because it was hastily built that day, but it was built for purpose and was ready for use. Even though servants had decorated the main support posts and along the main stage of the structure with fresh flowers and white linen it still looked ugly. Its presence was foreboding especially with the dangling, braided horse hair noose which was secured to an oak cantilever beam and swaying ominously in the gentle breeze.

Servants were still fussing over the center stage which sat lower than the hanging platform. It too was lavished in the same white cloth and cut flowers, but there was more effort put into its appearance. The edge of the white cloth was sewn with multiple rows of gold trim and highlighted by a thick maroon inlay of fabric. The flowers were more lavish, there were exotic orchids not from Kingsgate in huge clay urns. At the base of each urn to soften their dominant look were potted roses cut into topiaries of geometric shapes. At the center of the main stage was a podium with the finest hand sculptured marble of the royal crest, gold leaf inlay and encrusted with thousands of emeralds and diamonds.

And there it was in all its glory, the Crown Jewels. They sat on a maroon cushion on a single white marble column which stood at waist height. The gold on this crown was bright and the gems, which were tastefully arranged, were large and colourful. Because of its sheer weight and value it was only worn on special and important occasions. It had also been updated for this special occasion as Princess Margaret had to have a new and improved crown, she couldn't wear an outdated piece that her father had ruled in. Music played as invited guests started to enter the courtyard. Their eyes were averted towards the Crown Jewels, but

Princess Margaret needn't worry about their security as Lord James had placed two of the burliest guards Kingsgate had ever produced beside them.

Hundreds of large oval tables were also lavishly dressed in a similar motif to the main stage. Each table sat ten guests and each setting was adorned with fine bone china edged in gold with sterling silver cutlery. At the center of each table was a medium sized clay urn which also held a huge bloom of orchids that cascaded down the sides. Most of the guests hadn't seen such a grandiose display before, they sensed that this occasion was to be a momentous one. The tables were arranged towards the front of the courtyard adjacent to the main stage and hanging platform. This left plenty of open standing room at the back of the area for general town's folk. The town's folk weren't there to enjoy a meal, which was served during the coronation, but were there to bear witness to the official ceremony and hanging.

After all the important guests were seated, via correct placement from ushers, the general public were allowed to enter. Although they were held back from the seated guests by a long row of guards brandishing shields and swords they still felt important, they felt like they belonged. They had never been allowed this privilege before even under King Henry's rule.

The gentle music which was being played was beginning to lose its entertainment value as the wait was long and tiring. Those who were standing were getting boisterous and on occasion a guard had to leave the line and deal with an argument or fight. A couple of the revelers were ejected from the concourse, of course they would be spending quite some time to reflect upon themselves in the dungeon.

Suddenly all heads turned as trumpets blared signifying the entry of royalty. From the back corner of the courtyard a procession entered in single file headed by Lord James, followed by Lady Jane and her assistants, then chained by the ankle was Mary looking beautiful in her dress and being led by a guard in procession attire.

Mary radiated beauty. Her dress accentuated her figure, her hair had been styled with a Dutch braid and the single drop hung neatly between her shoulder blades. Intertwined into the top of her hair, in the shape of a casual tiara, was a ring of yellow daisies and baby's breath. She loved it when she was asked by Lady Jane's assistant to look into a mirror to make sure she was happy with the result. She also loved the fact that she was asked in the first place.

Mary carried herself quite well for someone who had one of the most terrifying days of her life. She still remembered petting Samuel this morning on the floor of her dungeon cell. She cringed as she still remembered being dragged by her hair from the guard, which still hurt her scalp as the hairdressers pulled her hair tight to form the braid. She didn't mind having a braid done but she still grimaced at the tenderness of her skin. From her confrontation with her sister, Princess Margaret, to her father's funeral, a man she never got to meet, to discovering her mother, Lady Jane to realizing her fate tonight, that she will be hung in front of everyone here. Mary should have been the princess, she carried herself with much better esteem even with the impending sacrifice for Princess Margaret's gratification. She followed the guard closely up a short set of stairs to the top of the main stage.

There she was asked to take her place with the other royalty at a long table which faced the on looking guests.

It wasn't long before a second round of trumpets were played. This time everyone knew Princess Margaret was to make her entrance, all stood. Heads were turned, bodies of those who were seated stretched forward and the standing public pressed against the line of guards who were now linking arms to hold them back. Without disappointment Princess Margaret's entrance was nothing less than a jaw dropping spectacle, gasps were heard radiating around the courtyard. She was led by two guards in full battle armor riding on black stallions. The gold plated armor reflected the courtyard torches. Behind them were four bronzed muscular men, much larger than the ones that delivered her dress earlier that day, wearing only gold plated armor from the waist down. The shadows rolled across their sculptured chests as they also marched past the torches. Their dramatic look was finished off with gold plated battle helmets which had black stallion tail hair tassels emanating from the top. They each carried the end of a large beamed platform which the princess rode upon. She turned her head slightly to capture the attention that she was receiving. She was in her element.

All eyes were not only on the procession as a whole but were on her dress. Nothing like it had ever been seen before. After alterations to make it lighter, Princess Margaret had insisted that a redesign was needed. She was too furious to wear that dress again. This time the gold chain dress was reinvented into a gold plate dress. The panels of the dress were made up of thin gold plates that were connected to adjacent plates by individual chain links. This way the panels followed the contours of her body and allowed her to move freely. This time the shape of the dress was more formal with an off the shoulder neckline, full length body with a leg split to also help her move freely. Her hair was free of the 'bird cage' look that she wore at the funeral and now she wore a simpler waterfall braid to accept the Crown Jewels during the coronation.

Not only were people staring at Princess Margaret's dress they were also fixated on the blue glowing orb hanging from a gold chain around her neck. Nobody except the royal party had seen such a thing before. The light radiating from the amulet was being reflected from her dress and the guard's gold plated suits and beams of light glinted into the crowd. Some people pointed at it, but quickly hid their hands as it was sacrilege to point at royalty, especially of the highest order. A lot of people looked dumbfounded, some were scared, as to what it was and what it may do. It added to Princess Margaret's spectacle.

Princess Margaret seemed to float above the crowd as she was transported to the main stage. The guards stopped alongside the front of the stage and Lord James assisted her in negotiating the gap between her platform and the stage. She thanked him, turned and gave the crowd a forced smile and a single hand wave. The crowd erupted with cheers and an awkwardly long round of applause, all of which Princess Margaret didn't seem to mind. She soaked it up.

Princess Margaret took her place at the head of the long table. Her immediate staff and Mary flanked her right and a crew of assistants, who ensured she was always looking her best were seated to her left. Her assistants fussed over her every move, the last thing she wanted was a dress malfunction. Lord James took position behind the podium, ready to commence proceedings. The guests at the tables took their seats.

"Welcome to a new beginning," boomed Lord James, which quietened the onlookers, "tonight we shall officially swear in the new queen. Tonight marks a change for our kingdom, a new hope. Tonight we shall celebrate, we shall feast and we shall be entertained." The guests again were upstanding, the cheers were deafening.

"Please welcome to the stage, Priest John," continued Lord James. The seated guests gently clapped as Priest John made his way across the front of the main stage to the side stairs. He promptly took position behind the podium as Lord James stood to the side of him and behind the Crown Jewels.

"It gives me great pleasure to join you in welcoming our new queen, I am honored to be bestowed the privilege through the hands of the Lord," began Priest John as he addressed the gathering, "please your majesty." He motioned for Princess Margaret to stand in between the podium and the Crown Jewels. Princess Margaret stood and made her way to the front of the stage, assistants closely followed her fussing over the placement of her dress and making necessary adjustments. Lord James moved to the side again giving her space.

"Please place your hand on the Holy Bible your royal highness," requested Priest John as he faced her holding out a leather bound bible in both hands. She removed a diamond studded glove and handed it to an assistant without looking at them, as though it was expected. "Your royal highness, with hand on the Lord's work, do you pledge to the allegiance that you solemnly swear to take ownership of Kingsgate and its people? Do you swear to protect, care and nurture through your leadership during famine and prosperity? Do you swear to rule with fairness and authority as though your birthright and your civic duty were one and the same? Do you swear to be honest to God and the King before you, so help you God?" The crowd was silent, waiting for Princess Margaret's response.

With a hand firmly on the bible Princess Margaret answered, "of course." She quickly removed her hand holding it out for the assistant to replace the glove.

"Then by the power vested in me by our Father almighty, I now declare that from this day forth you shall be Queen Margaret, ruler of the kingdom of Kingsgate," deemed Priest John. The crowd erupted, those that were seated stood up applauding with great gusto. The noise was deafening. The sound dulled slightly as all watched Lord James carefully pick up the Crown Jewels and gently place them on Queen Margaret's head. She turned to face the crowd and the standing ovation. Clapping, screams and cheers rumbled like a storm around the courtyard walls.

Queen Margaret stuck one arm out and motioning down for the noise to stop. The crowd shushed one another, 'Quiet, let the queen speak,' someone said and the cheering died down. The queen looked around at everyone. "Tonight I promised to show you, my people, that we will live in harmony and prosperity," cheers prematurely erupted again followed by more shushing. "Tonight we will celebrate, tonight we will feast on our good fortune," she continued looking around. "But," she shouted, "you the people have heard stories about the nature of my leadership. Lies I tell you," she explained, "in order for this kingdom to enjoy the fruits of our labor then sacrifices must be made. While you are feasting tonight, think about the sacrifices that were made for your freedom to be able to enjoy the food and wine. We all got here together under my family's rule. Never question my judgement and you will continue to live prosperously!"

The onlookers burst out cheering once more. Queen Margaret placed one arm out this time without movement. The noise ceased. "Before we feast, to uplift our spirits," she paused for dramatic effect, "we must sacrifice this swine!" she shouted and pointed directly at Mary. The guard behind Mary wrapped a burley arm around her neck reefing her up and backwards from her chair. Gasps, shouts and boos could be heard from the crowd as he carried her kicking and screaming to the hanging platform.

Chapter Twenty-One

The dungeon could best be described as an extreme environment, it was remarkable for anyone to have survived many years there. The winters were bitterly cold as the ground froze and the summers were unbearably hot and humid with little air flow for relief. Mary barely survived and was quite ill most of the time. Being extracted from the dungeon when she did was a blessing in disguise, even though she wouldn't have seen it that way with her impending public hanging. The same could be said for the release of another long term prisoner that day. His caged door was opened for his freedom, but the conditions of his release were strict.

While Mertane and Varn raced back to the castle that evening, on horseback through the forest that separated Shadow Valley to Kingsgate, he had been preparing himself for the important job that he had been given. His promised freedom gave him a steely resolve, he was determined to perform well. He couldn't believe his luck, his task was also the ability to act out revenge. It was handed to him on a silver platter. He took it with caution though and his mind raced for ideas on how to escape should the opportunity present, if everything turned sour.

He glanced over at the open cell caged door held back with a large rock and wondered if he should pick the rock up and strike the sole guard at the door. He thought against it as the rock was large and he was still weak from being undernourished. Besides he didn't know the layout of this castle and thought better of it as he didn't have the strength to face additional security unarmed.

Suddenly a clambering of what sounded like iron on iron and boots on steps were heard. It sounded like more troops were coming and their swords were striking their armor as they descended the dungeon stairs. The noise stopped and mumbling voices were heard before the noise turned away and he was left listening to moans and weeping from other prisoners. He thought himself lucky not to advance the guard with the rock, it would have been certain death.

"The prisoner must prepare," instructed the guard.

'This is it,' he thought to himself. Beside him a large wooden barrel sat off the floor, steam rose from the surface. It took courage for him not to jump into the water the minute it had been set up in his cell but he showed restraint. He slipped out of his heavily soiled poncho styled prisoner attire and slowly sank into the water. It felt invigorating. The hot water relieved his aching muscles, his bruised bones. He dunked his head underwater and screamed, the bubbles streamed upwards, rolling up his face, dashing past his tears. His anger, his fear and all the tension released into the hot bath along with the dirt from his filthy body.

"Out!" shouted the guard as he banged the side of the wooden bath with the butt of his sword. He gave the guard a scowl and promptly climbed over the edge of the bath. He didn't think he'd been in there very long, it wasn't enough time. He quickly put the black clothes on that he was given as the guard stood back outside the open cell door. The clothes were thick and heavy, 'so maybe he couldn't run very easy in them,' he thought. He wasn't surprised when he saw the black leather mask that was the last thing to put on. It is part of his attire as a hangman. A hangman always remained anonymous. He felt slightly begrudged as he wanted his victim to know who he was and all about his history. His revenge would feel sweeter that way. He slipped the full head piece on as instructed.

He gave his dungeon cell one last look over. It had been his shelter for the last sixteen years. For most of that time he hadn't left the confines of the four walls of the cell. He had done a stint of hard labor at the kingdom's quarry. That was short lived though as he was left maimed from other prisoners after they learnt who he was and attacked him. Now he would walk with a limp, but at least he would walk free. All he had to do was perform the ugly ritual of pulling the lever at the hanging station. A task which he would enjoy. It would be his rite of passage.

He held his arms up together at the guard, fists clenched. It was the usual practice before chains were wrapped around the wrists and a prisoner was led away. But not this time. "The prisoner will put its arms by its side," instructed the guard. "You will not be chained, you will follow me," the guard explained. "Be warned, from the towers our best archers will have their arrows trained for your heart." He nodded to indicate he understood what he was being told. "One thought of running, one step out of line and it will be your last," warned the guard.

He followed the guard closely, in a way shielding himself at the front, just in case an eager archer's finger slipped or all of a sudden got trigger happy. His scalp was valuable, the kill would have made the archer a hero in this kingdom. Even though he knew the princess would have disapproved at this point in time he thought his premature death would have been shrugged off. A 'mistake' would have been turned into a master stroke of planning. His mind still raced with any plan to escape, but it had to be a calculated one.

He was taken to a different section of the castle, one that he hadn't seen before. The narrow corridors concluded at a guarded steel barred gate which opened up to the courtyard gardens, right in the midst of a thick garden. They must have traversed a servant's tunnel. From here at the edge of the courtyard he heard the noise of people growing louder and louder as they pushed their way through thick garden pathways to the opening of the grand courtyard. There in front of them was the main stage, and there standing guarded beside the hanging noose was a blonde girl in full ballroom dress.

The guard who was leading him took out a small bladed dagger and changed positions to step behind him. He pushed the dagger firmly against his back, "remember what I said, run and you're dead, now up to that hanging platform," he said with a harsh hatred in his voice. "You may have been the king of your castle but in this kingdom the new queen is the only one who I'll bow to."

Chapter Twenty-Two

Trumpets again started blaring out a short cheerful tune to signify the commencement of proceedings as the masked hangman took his place beside the lever on the hanging platform. The guard that transported him there had left him unsecured but made him well aware of archers poised on each of the two turrets that overlooked the courtyard. He joined the three others that were standing on the platform, Queen Margaret, Mary and her guard still holding her chain. Lord James was not required on the stage as Queen Margaret was now in charge of proceedings, she didn't want anything to go wrong. All other royal family members, including Lady Jane and their assistants, were standing back down on the main stage, staring up in disbelief.

The heckling and jeering of the crowd subsided, they were now transfixed by the spectacle that was unfolding in front of them. It also didn't help that while they waited servants had loaded tables beside the stage with lavish assortments of food. Three whole roast pigs-on-a-spit were also carried out and hung up on a frame. It was a great ploy by the queen, to quieten down the crowd by ensuring the smell of food wafted past their noses. The only risk that now posed was a break out of revelers for the food. However the line of guards prevented this from happening.

Queen Margaret's amulet glowed even brighter and reflected around the courtyard off her multi-faceted gold plate dress. As she turned from left to right to take in the glory of her followers. The blue reflections appeared to twinkle in people's eyes. She heard the oohs and ahs and her smile beamed, she was loving the moment. Soon the peak of her euphoria would be realized. "Special guests, ladies and gentlemen," she started, shouting across the courtyard, "I thank you for joining me to witness a most wonderful event." She gestured towards Mary, "my first prisoner," she said and paused, "pardon me, our first prisoner," she corrected herself, "our first prisoner has the potential to ruin this kingdom." There were gasps and shushes around the courtyard. Many people found it hard to hear the queen and they pressed harder against the pack which placed a lot of pressure against the line of guards.

A caped wizard and his young apprentice entered the courtyard unnoticed by others who were all facing the hanging stage. "There Varn, there is Princess, err, Queen Margaret and that must be your sister, Mary," pointed out Mertane.

Look!" exclaimed Varn, who was amazed by the brightness of Mertane's amulet.

"Yes indeed Varn, I've never seen my amulet glowing so brightly, we must stop the queen before she makes a grave mistake," he said as he slipped the bright blue orb and its chain over his head. "Quick, take this to the stage, they must be joined to stop the curse, by all three of you with royal blood."

"Shouldn't you be calling me William now? That is who I truly am," pointed out Varn. "And where is Mary's amulet, I only see one on Queen Margaret?" he questioned.

"Let's keep your heritage under wraps for the moment, we don't want the queen to find out just yet, look what she's doing to your sister," Mertane pointed out. "And as for Mary's amulet, I don't know, let's hope she holds it, she may have it in her hands which seem to be tied behind her back," explained Mertane. "You run, quick, I'll try to catch up."

Varn pushed his way through the standing guests as Queen Margaret continued her speech, "for our Kingdom to remain strong, we can't have these imperfections, this disease. We must free ourselves of any forces which would place us in ruins and take our freedom!"

The courtyard guests broke out into cheers, screams and whistling, and then they started to chant, "the Queen is our savior, so God save the Queen." On and on they went, the queen was soaking it all up, "The Queen is our savior, so God save the Queen." She would have let them continue for quite some time except she noticed a blue glow making its way through the crowd towards the stage.

"Silence!" she screamed with her hands held out towards the revelers. There was utter silence as Varn made it to the line of guards. "State your name and where did you get that amulet?" barked Queen Margaret down towards the apprentice.

"I am Varn, apprentice wizard to your Master Wizard Mertane," explained Varn. She knew of Kingsgate's wizard Mertane but hadn't a great deal to do with him. As far as she knew he was an old stinky drinking buddy of her father, the late King Henry. She thought wizards were nothing but glorified magicians and she held little regard for them. "This amulet," continued Varn now holding it up towards the queen, "it was discovered in Shadow Valley." He lied.

"How intriguing, bring it up here at once," she spat. The guards let Varn pass their security line and he made his way up the side stair to the top of the hanging platform. It was quite a view from up there and Varn looked about the crowd, he couldn't see Mertane although he had little time to focus. He quickly glanced at Mary who was sobbing and trembling. He turned to face Queen Margaret who commanded his attention.

"Your interruption will earn you time in the dungeon, now hand it over to me, unless you want to join her," threatened the queen pointing to Mary with one hand and reaching for Varn's amulet with the other. Varn hesitated, he gave Mary a sympathetic look and then he looked back at the queen. "So you know this girl do you?" she said sensing there was something in the way that he looked at her, "give me the amulet, now, before I pull that lever myself!" she screamed pointing at the lever beside the hangman. Varn reluctantly gave her the amulet. He felt dejected. Varn had no idea of any magic, trick or plan that would see him in control of this situation. He hung his head in shame.

Queen Margaret took off her own amulet and held both of them together by the chains, they seemed to glow even brighter, to the point where she had to look away. "How intriguing," she said, "now your hesitation has earnt you second prize in the hanging competition. Watch and learn how she dies for it's your turn next."

"No!" yelled Varn. He lunged forward to try and knock Mary from the trap door that she was standing on, but as he did another blue orb seemed to jump from out of the shadows. A blackened shape, like a blur. It was Samuel. He had escaped the guards that had contained him earlier that evening. In Varn's sudden approach towards Mary an archer released a single arrow which cut through the air and sung like the flapping wings of a murder of crows. Samuel hissed and leapt up to shield Mary. The arrow missed Varn but firmly pierced Samuel's neck, smashing the amulet's chain and sending it flying, the poor cat dropped to the deck in a deathly thud. Queen Margaret caught Samuel's amulet in her empty hand. Now she had all three.

Before she could scream Mary felt the trap door beneath her give way. She was blinded by a quick succession of three flashes of brilliant white light. Her final memory as she felt her neck burn from the weight of the noose bite into her flesh, was of a loud crack.

Chapter Twenty-Three

Shades of light and dark flashed across her face, her eyes were open and she couldn't see anything but blurred shapes. She was lying in a comfortable bed but her body burned, she tried to turn her head but a stab of pain shot down the side of her neck. She tried to scream but a muffled noise came out of her mouth along with a stream of blood which rolled from the corner of her mouth, down the side of her cheek, and pooled on her pillow. She thought she heard voices like whispering nearby but she couldn't make out what was being said. As the ringing in her ears subsided she could just make out parts of the conversation.

"How's she doing?" somebody asked. She felt someone dabbing a cloth on her cheek to mop up the blood.

"Not well," was the reply, "time will tell."

She used up a lot of energy to listen to the voices. The last thing she thought she heard before she slipped into the dark void of unconsciousness again was the familiar soothing tones of a female's voice, "we all hope she makes it back, the kingdom needs their new leader."

It took Mary two more weeks to be able to see again. She hadn't shielded herself from the initial flash of the amulets explosion. As her body dropped through the opening in the hanging platform the explosion cut through the noose before her neck was broken. She had dropped harshly to the ground below the stage and wasn't found for hours. Now that her eyes were repaired she could see it was her mother, Lady Jane, who had set up a bedside vigil and had been tirelessly looking after her. She could see that she was in a grand bedroom and assumed she was in the royal chambers laying on the king's bed.

Most mornings, while Mary lay there helpless, she frustratingly practiced on improving her speech. Although the bleeding had stopped she still felt pain and could only manage single word sentences. This particular morning Lady Jane was wiping her down for her weekly bath. "Save your energy my love," Lady Jane said as she cleaned her forehead with a wet cloth. "You are safe now," she said, "now that you have more energy you should be strong enough to process some truths."

Mary turned her head and looked at Lady Jane in the eyes. "Yes?" she whispered.

"You'll be happy to know that your sister, well your step sister, is behind bars." Mary wondered how. How could she be safe from the blast of the amulets? "And I know what you are thinking with that furrow on your face," explained Lady Jane. "Margaret was protected by her gold plate dress. She was found unconscious on the ground. She was cared for under guard, but she mended quite quickly and was taken under kingdom arrest." Lady Jane further explained that it was deemed under civic meetings that Queen Margaret broke her oath pledged under her coronation. She was stripped of her royal duties and under majority vote by council leaders determined her to be of ill mind and a threat to the future of the kingdom.

"You are next in line to the throne, my love," Lady Jane explained with a smile. "It's all too much to take in now but in due time, when you have healed, the right to refuse the position of queen is yours." Mary was exhausted, she held Lady Jane's hand and drifted off to sleep.

It wasn't until that evening that Mary woke again. "You have a visitor," explained Lady Jane. "You haven't met him before but he means you no harm, he's the kingdom's wizard, Master Wizard Mertane." He approached with his hat off but still wore his heavy cloak. His eyes looked over Mary's weak body sorrowfully. "I'll give you a minute alone," said Lady Jane, "he says he has something important to tell you. Don't worry I'll be just outside the door." Lady Jane gently closed the state room door behind her.

Mary tried to keep her eyes on his towering silhouette but she grew tired and rolled on her back looking up at the ceiling. Mertane cleared his throat, "my assistant and I were in a race to save the princess that day, we weren't aware that she was greedy and desperate to rule the kingdom. Her abuse of power was extraordinary." He continued to explain, "we were in a rush to save her, but along the way we found out about you."

"And," Mary whispered.

"Yes, and had I known that you were in the dungeon all those years then I personally would have rescued you," stated Mertane.

"Why?" she asked.

"It's a long story Mary, or should I say Princess Mary?" he said.

"Please?" she asked.

"Lady Jane said to keep it brief, so I will. When you are better we can go over your whole heritage," he explained. "I came here to tell you a pleasant secret that Lady Jane doesn't even know. It should uplift your spirits."

"Yes?" she said.

"It turns out that you have a brother, William, who was hiding here in the kingdom all along," explained Mertane, "he's quite a character, I am sure you'll get along with him very well."

"Samuel?" she asked.

"The cat?" queried Mertane.

"Yes," she replied.

"I am afraid you'll never see him again. He lost too much blood and we couldn't save his frail body."

Mary rolled on her side turning her back to Mertane. She buried her face into the soft mattress. She didn't want him to see her uncontrollable tears and her infinite sadness. Mertane quickly left the room, he couldn't bear to see her in any more pain.

Chapter Twenty-Four

She wished her memories of the last couple of weeks were only a nightmare and not reality. She wished she woke to Samuel rubbing his body against her side. Nothing could bring him back now, no amount of tears, no amount of screaming. Mary's mind repeated over and over the events of that fateful night. Samuel had spared her life by sacrificing his own. She wished he hadn't and she wished she was the one buried here on this open meadow overlooking the reaching patchwork quilt of farmland in the floor of Shadow Valley.

Samuel's fresh grave was unmarked and unnoticeable, which was the way Mary wanted it. She didn't want anyone else to know he was buried here. His life had been taken tragically and she didn't want anybody to be able to disturb him while he rested here in peace. So many secrets had been kept from her, this was her own secret. This would be her own quiet place, to rest and reflect and to share time with Samuel.

She pushed the long strands of her hair behind her ears as the gusts of wind whipped them about her face. She thought Samuel's grave looked bare so she got up and wandered to the edge of the meadow, to where the wild flowers grew the most densely. As she picked the flowers she dared to think of what her life may now entail, and tears again streamed from her eyes as she couldn't think of a future without Samuel. They had been together for so long, they had been one another's shining light and kept each other going in the darkest moments of their lives. Now that light had been extinguished.

She made her way back to Samuel's plot, kneeling beside it with her face pointing towards the direction of the wind so that her hair remained kempt. She gazed at the flowers' beauty with a vacant stare. She wondered if the butterfly, whose wing that she had tossed in the breeze, had visited these flowers. She wondered if Samuel would have liked being here in the meadow, jumping in and out of the thickets, stalking her and tackling her legs mischievously as they wasted time together on a glorious day like this. "Here you go Samuel, I hope you love them," she said as she placed the bunch of flowers on top of the earth mound and held them down by resting a small stone over their stems.

"I do love them," a male's voice said from behind her.

Mary quickly spun around and reared a clenched fist. She could only make out a dark silhouette shape as the sun was eclipsing the back of his head. She squinted as she questioned aggressively, "who are you?"

"Sorry please forgive me, I didn't mean to scare you, I am William, your brother," he explained, still standing there. "I know you've been through a lot and we haven't properly met but I feel I've known you, well, forever."

"What do you mean forever?" she questioned, still squinting and now holding a hand over her eyes to shade them from the sun. She still couldn't make out his face and wished he'd move so that she could get a better look at him. "Aren't you Mertane's assistant and didn't you only just discover that you were really my brother William?"

"Now I am the confused one," answered William as he moved a few paces to the side of Mary. Now Mary could get a good look at his face.

"Yes, you are William who was known as Varn," she explained as she recognized his face from that fateful night. "You were up there on the hanging platform. You brought Margaret an amulet. You also tried to save me." Mary stood now and walked over to William.

"I don't know who Varn is," said William, "but I was on that hanging platform."

"What?" said Mary frustrated, "you're not making any sense?"

"You see Mary, when the amulets were brought together a curse was broken," said William as he approached Mary holding out his hand in front of him. He held onto Mary's hands and she let him as they looked into each other's eyes, "and with the curse broken so too I was released from my own prison."

"What prison was that?" questioned Mary as her hands began to tremble.

"I was trapped in the body of a cat," he said. Mary's lip now quivered and her eyes began to welt. "When I was transformed many years ago, I searched and I found you in the castle dungeon. You called me Samuel." Mary let go of his hands and wrapped her arms around him. Mary sobbed into his chest and didn't let him go.

"After the explosion, and when I saw that you were safely being cared for I came back here to Shadow Valley to explain everything I knew to our parents that brought us up." he explained. "You were very little when I was transformed and when you were taken, you probably don't remember them, they were good people, our parents," he said thinking back to his childhood as he looked over towards the farms below.

"How do you know so much?" questioned Mary, still holding onto William.

"As a cat I was able to roam freely," he explained. "I was able to see things and to hear things that I wouldn't have been able to as a human. But I am still trying to piece some of the things together that don't make sense."

It felt like an eternity had passed when Mary finally let him go and looked into his eyes. "So if you are my brother William, who was trapped in Samuel, then who is Varn?" she questioned.

"That I don't know," replied William, "but it sounds like we had better find out."

Chapter Twenty-Five

Constant moaning and muffled sobs along with screams from rats fighting kept her awake through the night. Her skin and hair was dirty and itchy, she hadn't had a bath in two weeks. Her rage was strong but she was growing weaker by the day. She hated everyone and everything but most of all she hated that she was still alive. If she could kill someone she would. If she could kill something, anything, she would. It might have given her some satisfaction. She wasn't broken yet and her resolve kept her alive but she feared she would go crazy before she could get her revenge.

Margaret lay on her back on a wooden frame bed with a thin hessian bag for padding. Her back ached from laying there but she didn't want to move. She lay there stewing in her hatred. She couldn't believe that the amulets were cursed and that bringing all three together ended the curse in a final, deadly explosion. It was like a trap had been set. Although it didn't kill her like it was supposed to it had ruined her plans of power. She even trusted King Charles from Brookhaven with the role of hangman. How stupid of her. She didn't learn of what happened to him, maybe he escaped. She hoped he was blown to smithereens.

She heard footsteps approaching but she just kept looking up at the ceiling. They stopped outside her cell. "I see you are enjoying yourself," taunted the voice.

"Who are you?" Margaret snapped, "let me see your face." The visitor purposely moved into the light of a nearby wall mounted torch and the light and shadows flickered across his face. He was a young man in his late teenage years with patchy facial hair that stood out on his pale face. His medium black straight hair was tied back.

"Oh it's you," she said unimpressed. "I thought that arrow killed you on the platform?" She rolled back to her lying position unimpressed by his presence.

"No it missed," he said matter-of-fact, "that arrow killed the cat."

"Good, at least one thing went right that night," Margaret said. She always found animals repulsive. They could never be controlled and they always stunk. "What was your name again?" she asked.

"Varn," he responded.

"What do you want?" she asked.

"I want to offer you your freedom for your planned revenge. I am sure you have thought about it, you've had enough time," he said. "You might enjoy it, who knows you might be queen again someday?"

"How do you propose that I seek my revenge, do you see an army of followers here in my cell? You are only an apprentice child wizard after all," she said.

"This is my guise," he explained placing both of his arms out beside himself and bobbing down quickly on bent knees, like a bowing stage performer would at curtain call, "my real name is Wizard Jotane of Brookhaven."

"What?" she said, cutting him off, "didn't daddy put you in prison when you and King Charles tried to conquer our kingdom?" She sat up now, the wooden bed frame creaked with the shift of weight. She was intrigued and he had her undivided attention now.

"Yes I was in prison here many years ago, that was after your father stole the amulets from our kingdom and made me give them power to protect him and his family," he explained.

"So you are responsible for the amulets!" she shrieked.

"Yes of course, I placed a curse on them because my life was destroyed. Serves your father right for not getting his own wizard to do his work," he explained. "I used magic to stage my death and transform myself into a helpless boy who would become the nephew of the great wizard Mertane." Her eyes remained on him as he continued to explain, "After all, where else would an enemy wizard feel safer than with a fellow wizard, oh the secrets and tricks I learnt there!"

"But the amulets, they blew up before me, they nearly killed me!" she shouted.

"Yes that was the plan. When your father was still alive and ruling, the curse was working to make his life a living hell. He would watch his family slowly become damaged or die. Much like King Charles and I witness in our kingdom of Brookhaven under the hand of your father. His death triggered the time bomb that the amulets ultimately were, the catalyst of which was when they were all brought together by the last of the three royal family members," Jotane explained.

"Three?" she questioned, her anger levels were starting to rise again, "what do you mean, there is only Mary and I. Who is the other and do tell me Mary's neck was snapped."

"Mary is alive and well, and her brother, your step brother William is alive too. I haven't seen him since the amulets exploded that night, but he is alive," he explained.

"What do you mean step brother?" she demanded an explanation.

"He is Mary's twin brother and was also sent to hide in Shadow Valley when he was born. You didn't know about him because I changed him into a black cat, the ultimate bad luck charm that I could think of at the time, before you captured and imprisoned Mary" he said, "and both Mary and William are of King Henry's blood."

"But I am of his blood too, the very thing you and King Charles despise," she said, "what's stopping you from destroying me once you have the revenge that you seek?"

"Your blood you could say is, well, bad blood, and I have a feeling that once we destroy the rest of your family and finally conquer Kingsgate then we will get on remarkably well," he said as he griped the bars of the dungeon cell door. His hands started to glow a blue aura and the lock on the gate smashed and fell to the floor.

"Yes," Margaret said with a wry smile, "I like what you're feeling."

Epilogue

The seasons raced by quickly and not before too long winter had covered the land with a thick blanket of snow. Mary stood out on one of the castle terrace balconies which faced Shadow Valley looking over the expanse of white. She could just make out the tops of the valley cliff walls in the distance. She shivered as a gentle breeze brushed across her cheeks causing her skin to tighten and blush. Mary pulled her thick lamb's wool lined cloak closer to her body by crossing her arms and wrapping them around her torso.

She gazed out into winter's day as she wondered what happened to her sister and how far Kingsgate had come along since her freedom. Mary knew it must have been Jotane, disguised as Varn, that had freed Margaret from the dungeon but everybody she questioned could not tell her a thing. Although Mary was still undecided on becoming Queen of Kingsgate she made it her very first duty as princess to interview each and every prisoner in the dungeon. She wanted to know if they had seen anything the day Margaret had escaped, she wanted to know why they were incarcerated in the first place but most of all she wanted to know, by staring at them directly in their eyes, if they were innocent of any wrongdoing.

The tears of joy flowed the day when prisoner upon prisoner were assisted out of the dark cells, along the dim passageways and out into the bright light of freedom. Guards which once taunted Mary now helped her by tearing down the hanging platform. Stonemasons and guards worked alongside each other and painstakingly boarded up Mary's old cell, stone by stone. It would now be a constant reminder, a monument, that no living soul would be unjustly imprisoned.

Both William and Mary spent many days out at the maize farm with their surrogate parents, Thomas and Elizabeth, going over all they knew about their childhood. Piecing together the timeline of events over a cup of warm herbal tea, after many tears and hugs they surmised that it must have been Varn that turned William into a black kitten when he was about two years old and then he took William's identity, injecting himself into the life of Mertane's sister as a toddler. The exact moment when the black kitten, William, became Mary's pet, Samuel, was unknown because both

Thomas and Elizabeth were understandably distracted by the loss of their son. Margaret was ten years older than the twins and it was around her sixteenth birthday that she discovered that she had a hidden stepsister. She devoted all her energy to finding Mary and to have a band of well paid-off villagers capture her. She didn't even need her father's permission to imprison Mary as Margaret lied about her first captor's identity and the reason for incarceration. At the time King Henry was proud of Margaret.

But one of the hardest hit after all of the fallout was Mertane. Mary had visited his den many times over the months that had passed to console him and to confide in him. They both helped each other with their losses. Varn had been such a huge part of Mertane's life even if at times it was hard to live with the boy and the generational gap that divided their ways. It was hard for Mertane to now look at William, all he could see was Varn, but he knew it wasn't Varn. Jotane used powerful premonition spells to see into the future how William would have looked as a young man, the strength of such a spell baffled Mertane. He couldn't believe the stark contrast in personalities between William and Varn, but figured it was good that there was a difference because it freed Mertane of showing any resentment towards William. Mertane had loved Varn and it pained him to think that underneath that skin, under the guise lurked a truly evil being in Jotane. That was what kept Mertane from sleeping, he couldn't stop thinking about how he didn't know, how he couldn't feel that it was all a trick. Mertane's only resolve now, with Mary's encouragement, was to hone his sorcery, to grow personally and to grow physically as one of the most powerful wizards of all time. Mertane was tired, the road ahead for him looked as grey and foreboding as the thick clouds that were now rolling in from over Shadow Valley, but his determination for resolve kept him going.

Even though William and Mary had now each other it still took a long time for both of them to adjust to one another. Lady Jane was the glue which held them together and encouraged them to lead the kingdom. Lady Jane was blessed that her children listened to her and stood by her side. She held high hopes that Kingsgate would be brought back to its former glory. Lady Jane still worried over her children and when Mary would go missing from Kingsgate she would smile to herself as she got the word back from her most trusted assistant that she was once again basking in the sun in a flower meadow in Shadow Valley.

As snow started to fall Mary lifted a lamb's wool lined hood piece over her head to protect herself. She placed both hands on the cold stone terrace balustrade, she felt the cold of the stone slowly numbing her fingers. She flinched as a pair of arms wrapped around her shoulder to keep her warm, but she kept facing the view. Even though she knew it was William's loving embrace it would take her some time, if not an eternity, to become used to any affection from anyone. Her time spent in the dungeon had taken its toll. The scars were too deep.

"Beautiful view, isn't it?" asked William.

"Yes, it's a beautiful landscape," she replied.

"Do you think one day we might find peace here?" he asked, rubbing her shoulders with his sturdy hands trying to keep her warm.

"Let's hope so," replied Mary with a smile as she let go of the balustrade and placed one of her hands on his hand.

"We should head inside Mary, a big storm is on its way," he warned.

"Yes, yes it is," she answered, still staring blankly across the land, "and we will be ready for it."

oOo

Acknowledgments

First and foremost, I give my wholehearted thanks to my wife – my greatest critic – for her unbiased review, unconditional support and tireless proofing.

I would also like to thank you, the reader, for letting me share my fiction with you – and I hope you enjoyed the journey.

About the author

Leon Jane has always liked reading stories with a twist or with hidden messages, perhaps it stems from being a Gemini or that he loves being creative. He likes to delve into his imagination by creating stories and poetry which cover various genre. When he's not busy reading or writing he loves spending time in his tropical garden with his beautiful family in Far North Queensland, Australia.